BAD
MANNERS

CLARKSON N. POTTER, INC./
PUBLISHERS

DISTRIBUTED BY
CROWN PUBLISHERS, INC.
NEW YORK

BAD
MANNERS

A NOVEL BY

MAGGIE
PALEY

Published by Clarkson N. Potter, Inc., 225 Park
Avenue South, New York, New York 10003 and
simultaneously in Canada by General Publishing
Company Limited
CLARKSON N. POTTER, POTTER, and colophon are
trademarks of Clarkson N. Potter, Inc.

Manufactured in the United States of America

Library of Congress Cataloging-in-Publication Data
Paley, Maggie.
    Bad manners.

    I. Title.
PS3566.A4628B3   1986   813'.54   85-25732
ISBN 0-517-55998-6

10 9 8 7 6 5 4 3 2 1

First Edition

FOR
MY
MOTHER
AND
FATHER

Principal Characters

VIOLET   A publicist.

HELENA   A wife; formerly an assistant design curator.

ALEXANDRA   A radio personality.

KITTY   Proprietor of Luxury Foods, Ltd.

JOHN   Helena's husband; a book publisher.

PHILIP   Violet's boyfriend; a scientist.

GIORGIO   An Italian playboy.

HENRY SWEET   Proprietor of the Sweet School of Human Possibility.

ROGER RATHBONE   A movie star.

Others

JUDY THAXTER   A *Gossip* magazine reporter.

RITA   Violet's daughter; a student.

FREDDY   Violet's boss.

HELENA'S MOTHER

Violet called Helena from her desk at Star-Time Public Relations on Monday morning. "I didn't wake you up, did I?" Violet said energetically. She uncovered the Styrofoam cup on her gray metal desk with the overflowing gray metal in-box on it and took a sip of tepid tea with milk. As breakfast the tea was unsatisfactory, bringing to mind all her other unfulfilled desires.

"I've been up for hours," said Helena, who didn't like anyone to get ahead of her.

"That's good," Violet said. "I just called Elvira Dinwiddie and woke her up."

"You woke up Elvira Dinwiddie?"

"We're handling her new play, *Smoke and Fire*. She asked me to call her early this morning. So I called at nine-thirty, and I must have interrupted a bad dream. I said, 'You wanted to talk early.' She said, 'Darling, in my bedroom it's still the middle of the night.' You know me, I started to imagine other people in the bed with her. John Richards, he's playing her husband and Nigel Underhill, he's her lover. I got off the phone so fast I still don't know what she wanted."

"You must have been embarrassed for her," Helena said. "It's a good rule never to call anyone you don't know very well before ten in the morning or after eight at night."

Helena thought she was entitled to lay down rules of etiquette for her friends because she'd been so well brought up. Violet hated to be told what to do. "Yes dear," she said. "Now I want your opinion about something. It won't take long."

"If it won't take long, I guess it's not about Philip."

"Don't be fresh. I'm going to have a dinner party two weeks from Saturday."

"Yes?" Helena said.

"I want to invite Harriet Adams, but I've already had her to dinner twice and she's never invited me. The thing is, she's a good friend of Gordon Blair, and the party's for Gordon. And besides, Philip likes her and he isn't attracted to her."

"You know Philip isn't attracted to anyone but you, but why not invite her? Maybe she doesn't *have* people to dinner," Helena said.

"You're right. I thought I'd invite Elliot Ames, too. Or is it Ames Elliot? I'm so bad with names. The man I'm interested in from White's Bank."

"The stuffy one? How's he going to like Gordon's dirty stories? And doesn't Harriet always bring her own marijuana?"

Violet swiveled her chair around to look out on Madison Avenue. Last week's translucent pink azaleas were dying in a corner of her windowsill. She picked a blossom and tore it into tiny strips. "Maybe I can ask Harriet not to bring her marijuana," she said. "After all, she owes me a favor."

"She doesn't ask you to ask her to dinner, does she? There's no big sigh of relief when she hears your voice on the phone? She's just leading her own life when you call. What kind of favor does she owe you?"

Sometimes Violet wanted to kill Helena. "I think I'll hold off on Ames," she said. "Do you think I should invite the Duffys? The Weiners are going to the Galapagos Islands."

"The geraniums on my terrace need watering," Helena said. "Why don't you discuss the party with Harriet Adams or someone else who's going to be there?"

"Oh, Helena," Violet said very reasonably, "it's not your kind of party. You don't like Gordon Blair or his work."

"I'd better go now and make plans for what John and I will do for dinner two weeks from Saturday," Helena said.

"Thanks for your help," Violet said. She hoped that wasn't real anger she'd heard in Helena's voice. She drank the last of her awful tea and decided to think about it tomorrow.

Under ordinary circumstances, Helena would have said it was terribly inconsiderate to tell one friend about another friend's party. But the circumstances weren't ordinary when she called Alexandra on Tuesday afternoon.

"Helena, darling, you've been on my mind all day." Alexandra was using the sultry yet compassionate voice she used when people called in for advice on her radio show. She sounded as if she were in bed with someone, thinking about the problem at hand. "I had a dream last night that a friend of mine was having twins by two different fathers," she said.

"It couldn't have been me. I happen to know I didn't get pregnant again this month," Helena said. "Have you talked to Violet lately?"

"No, darling, is she acting up?"

"Then she didn't invite you to her party for Gordon Blair two weeks from Saturday. She's inviting Harriet Adams, even though she hardly knows her."

"Gordon and I are good friends." Alexandra sounded wistful.

"Well, she didn't invite me either, but at least she didn't call you and ask you who she should invite."

"I hope Gordon isn't mad at me," Alexandra said. "I missed his last show."

"Friends can't always invite each other everywhere, of course." Helena sat up straight and crossed her legs at the ankles like a mature woman. Her chair was a perfect reproduction of a 1924 high-backed armchair with red and yellow flowered upholstery. "I kept my temper on the phone," she said. "But now it seems to me Violet was rubbing it in. What do you think?"

"Definitely. She was rubbing it in. Is there some reason she's mad at you?"

"I told her I'm sick of Philip. I mean, not him, but her agonizing over him."

"Poor Violet," Alexandra said. "It makes her problem seem real to have someone else worrying about it with her."

Helena stopped to consider this. "I guess I'm willing to miss a party if it means I can worry less about her problem," she said. She felt relieved and began to file her nails. "Speaking of problems, how's Giorgio?"

"That's a good question." Alexandra sighed. "He's been

calling me three times a day. I don't think I want to go to Milano and meet his sister and marry him. I wouldn't even talk to him on the phone, but I'm very attracted to his voice. He's a millionaire, too. It's like a joke someone's playing on me, that all he cares about is material things. I need a man who has a higher purpose in life. I have to ask the *I Ching* about him."

"That's a book you throw coins at, right?"

"It's a book of ancient Chinese wisdom. You toss three coins six times to find out which hexagram you're supposed to read. There are sixty-four hexagrams. Each one is a little piece of advice."

Helena said, "Isn't it something hippies used to use?"

"Hippies used it, brilliant psychiatrists used it—it always tells you to do the right thing and everything will be all right."

Helena used her right hand to brush fingernail dust off her skirt. "My mother told me that," she said.

"Of course, darling," Alexandra said, "but did she know what the right thing was?"

"Does *it?*"

"Your unconscious mind speaks to you through it. Your unconscious mind always knows what's good for you, and when you toss the coins it tells you, that's all."

"It sounds so complicated," Helena said. "Wouldn't it be simpler just to talk to Giorgio? Tell him you don't want to marry him and he shouldn't call you anymore."

"That would be cruel. It hurts me to be cruel," Alexandra said softly.

"You know what they say," Helena said. "Sometimes you have to be cruel to be kind."

"I'm going to call Gordon right away," Alexandra said. "It's my fault we've been out of touch."

• • •

Before she called Gordon, Alexandra called Kitty at her food store, Luxury Foods, Ltd. "Kitty, darling, how are you?" she said. She fluffed up her hair with both hands, picturing, in her mind's eye, a glowing brown halo, and tucked her feet under her on the bed.

"I was out dancing late last night," Kitty said.

"Poor darling," Alexandra said. Kitty was always telling you what a great life she had. "Are you going to Violet's party for Gordon Blair?"

"She hasn't invited me yet. When is it?"

"Two weeks from Saturday. I'm not invited either. I didn't go to his last opening. Do you think he's mad at me?"

"I went. You didn't miss much," Kitty said. "Gordon looked great. The paintings were the same as last year's, only it was oranges instead of grapes. Apples, oranges, and French breads. Perfectly fine but, you know, I look at French breads all day long. The crowd was mostly Gordon's gay friends and freeloaders. I only stayed fifteen minutes. I didn't see anything there I wanted to do. I sent Gordon a funny note, though. I'm sure I'll be invited."

"Helena's not invited. Harriet Adams is. Violet invited Giorgio but he turned her down on my account." Though Alexandra didn't know this last to be a fact, she felt the spirit to be true.

"Then you're still seeing Giorgio?"

Alexandra leaned back on her soft pillows and picked up the glass globe paperweight that always sat on her bedside table. When you turned the globe upside down and back, snow fell on the pink and green Turkish palace inside. Snow globes reminded Alexandra that you couldn't count on anything in life.

Otherwise she wouldn't be talking to Kitty about Giorgio when she'd intended not to. Kitty always wanted to know all the boring details about Giorgio if you gave her any opening. "I asked the *I Ching* what to do with him," Alexandra said.

"What did it say?"

"I got the hexagram Retreat. It said, 'Retreat is a sign of strength.' It said to be careful not to miss the right moment."

"What does that mean?" Kitty said.

"I'm not sure, to tell you the truth. The thing about the *I Ching* is, it all depends on how you interpret it. Retreat should mean leave him, but the hexagram also says retreat is only a temporary step, before another forward movement. I don't think I want to leave him so that I can get him back again later."

"I wouldn't mind having a man like Giorgio," Kitty said.

"No, you wouldn't like him." Kitty was a good businesswoman because she was incredibly greedy. "I thought you were after that editor Helena introduced you to, the one John just brought over from England," Alexandra said.

"Anthony. I think he's gay. Helena says Rebecca told her."

"It's amazing the way she trusts Rebecca, considering how often John works late, isn't it, darling?" Alexandra said, sadly shaking her head. "I would give Anthony a chance if I were you. All Englishmen are a little gay. Otherwise they'd be too stuffy."

"At least he's not American. All American men are clods," Kitty said.

Alexandra sat up. "Darling. Come with me after work tonight," she said. "I'm going to visit my agent Harvey's father in the hospital. He's a very suave Czech."

Kitty said, "Can you hold on for a minute?" and put Alexandra on hold. Alexandra tried to picture Kitty with Harvey's father. He knew everything about Czech cuisine. She would walk too fast for him. "That was this evening's dinner plans," Kitty said, coming back on the line. "Now, did you say you've got a sick old man you think I'm going to fall in love with?"

"It's only a kidney stone," Alexandra said. "Why do I get so depressed when I have to visit someone in the hospital?"

"I don't know," Kitty said. "You don't have to stay more than twenty minutes. Just tell him a few funny stories."

"Twenty minutes. That's not bad. I hope it doesn't hurt when he laughs." Alexandra felt so much better she stopped thinking about herself. "Now, tell me what else is going on with you, darling," she said tenderly.

"Do you want to hear about the divine new pasta dish we're introducing?"

"No, please, I'm fasting today."

"You'll love this," Kitty said. "It's linguine with chocolate sauce. It saves calories because it's a main dish and a dessert at the same time. When did you say Violet was having her party?"

"Two weeks from Saturday."

"I think I'll have a party that night and invite her," Kitty said. "Maybe I'll serve linguine with chocolate sauce. I'll let you know. *Ciao.*"

Kitty believed in sleeping on her decisions, so she didn't call Violet until the following evening. She had decided to make Violet her confidante in spite of her well-known difficulty in keeping a secret.

"I don't know what to do about Giorgio," Kitty said. She

was in her white silk bathrobe at her dressing table, putting the last coat of fuchsia polish on her toenails.

"Giorgio?" There was a note of alarm in Violet's voice. "Giorgio who?"

"Giorgio you know who. I met him at your place. He's been phoning me three times a day for a week now. I think he's cute."

"So does Alexandra. He calls her three times a day, too," Violet said.

"She told me yesterday she wants to ease him out of her life. Do you think he's a womanizer?"

"That's hard to say. Maybe he just hasn't found Miss Right yet."

"Would Alexandra be mad at me if I went out with him, do you think?" Kitty dabbed a small streak of polish on the soft pad of her right big toe by mistake.

"Yes," Violet said.

"What should I do?"

"I suppose Helena would say the right thing to do is to tell him you can't see him while he's still involved with Alexandra. Then again I never do the right thing. Maybe that's why I'm so miserable all the time."

Kitty recognized the whiny tone. Violet was having romantic longings for Philip, and would feel better if she talked about him. On the whole she seemed happier talking about him than being with him. "How's Philip?" Kitty said.

"The usual, only worse than usual. He says he's not sure he's in love with me."

"Didn't you tell him you didn't love him last week?" Kitty said.

"Yes, but I had a good reason," Violet said. "I didn't like the way he was flirting with Alexandra."

Kitty put the top back on her polish. She soaked a small

cotton ball in polish remover and began her favorite phase of any job, the inspection and cleanup. It was then she got to appreciate her handiwork. "Philip may have had a good reason, too," she said.

Violet said, "If he's not in love with me there's certainly no point moving in with him."

"Who says you have to move in with him?"

"He does, sometimes. I've told you that."

"Then he must love you."

"He doesn't insist enough," Violet said. "I know if I died he could live without me. I don't call that true love."

Kitty said, "I think you and he enjoy fighting with each other."

"Do you think so? That's interesting." The introduction of a new line of speculation always calmed Violet, and made it possible to change the subject.

"I think I'll have a party and invite Alexandra and Giorgio and see what happens," Kitty said.

"That's a great idea. I wouldn't miss it," Violet said.

Kitty put down the polish remover and opened her big black appointment book where she'd already penciled in the date. "I'll have it two weeks from Saturday," she said.

"Two weeks from Saturday," Violet said.

"Can you come?"

"Two weeks from Saturday?" Now it was Violet's turn to sigh. "I was going to have a party for Gordon Blair that night. But it's causing me a lot of trouble. I think Helena's mad at me, and I haven't been able to get Gordon on the phone so I don't even know if he can make it. Maybe I'll cancel my party and go to yours instead. It will be much easier on my nerves."

Kitty said, "Okay, I'll count you in. Now, tell me why you think Helena's mad at you."

"I called her to confer about the guest list. I thought she'd enjoy it. She'd have a chance to tell me how to do things. She said, 'Why don't you discuss it with someone who's going to be there?'"

"You mean you asked her to help plan the party and you didn't invite her? She *should* be mad at you," Kitty said.

"Really? Oh, God, what can I do?"

"You could apologize."

"Thanks, Kitty," Violet said. "You'll have to come when I have my party for Gordon."

"I'd love to." Kitty smiled at herself in her dressing table mirror. "Next time we meet, remind me I have an interesting tidbit for you," she said. "It's about John Welles and Rebecca."

"Tell me right now. We won't meet until Saturday afternoon."

"Right now my doorbell is ringing," Kitty said. "Anthony's here and I'm not dressed."

"Anthony?"

"That new English editor Helena introduced me to. I think he's gay," said Kitty, and she hung up and went to the door in her robe.

Violet took a twenty-minute walk, recalling all the things she loved about Helena, before she phoned her. Helena sounded cool. Violet wished she would say she was angry, if she was. "Listen," Violet said, "I shouldn't have asked you to help me with a party I wasn't inviting you to. I'm sorry. It's just that you always know who goes with what."

"Thanks for seeing it from my point of view," Helena said.

"It's too bad. I want to insist that you come to the party now," Violet said, "but I've decided to cancel it."

"That is too bad," Helena said. "I could have taken another good look at you and Philip together. Then I might have been able to say something intelligent the next time you brought him up."

"You're a good friend when you want to be," Violet said.

"So are you," said Helena.

TWO

Kitty was jumpy when she called Helena in the middle of the next week to ask for advice. "Did I tell you I'm going to introduce linguine with chocolate sauce at my party on Saturday?" she said.

"Oh," Helena said, "it's a promotional party. I thought it was for your friends." Her voice trailed off as if she'd just suffered a terrible disappointment.

"Of course it's for my friends. I want them to be the first to taste it. And anyway," Kitty said gleefully, in spite of the pains she took to sound nonchalant, "the *Gossip* reporter said it would be good for her story if I introduced it at the party."

"What *Gossip* reporter?"

"Oh, dear. I hope I haven't done the wrong thing." Kitty opened her eyes up wide as if she were on a picture phone and Helena could see her consternation. Three brown cows on a green hillside looked back at her evenly from the big photograph on the wall opposite her desk. As a little girl her ambition had been to have rich dairy farmers as parents. "A reporter from *Gossip* called me on Monday. They want to do a piece about me. I don't know why," she said. "The reporter said their readers would like to know what rich people eat. Well, why shouldn't they? A story in *Gossip* could be worth a lot of money to me."

"So you invited the *Gossip* reporter to your party?"

Kitty happened to know Helena read *Gossip*. She had no right to get angry because other people made their living writing it. "Do you think inviting her to my party was in bad taste?" she said. "She sounds very nice."

"My mother would never have invited a *Gossip* reporter to a party at her house. Then again, my mother's a snob."

"The truth is," Kitty came to the point, "I wish I could ask your mother how to handle a *Gossip* reporter. I don't want to come off like one more farm girl from the Midwest."

"Poor Kitty," Helena said, as if someone had asked her to compromise her own principles. "People ought to be able to live their lives without having to worry about the impressions they're making on some journalist."

"Are you kidding? Do you think I'd rather Georgina Sherman at Food Paradise was the one who had this problem? I'm in business to make money."

Helena didn't speak. Violet always said Helena's telephone silences were hostile. Listening to the dead air, Kitty liked to imagine she could hear the sound of Helena changing her mind. "Okay," Helena said after a full minute. "Please don't call my mother. She'll just call me, wanting to know why no one's ever done a story on me. I'll tell you what she'd do with a *Gossip* reporter. She wouldn't talk about money."

Kitty said, "That attitude makes me mad. Everyone who works, works for money."

"Not at the museum they don't."

"The museum is a bad example," Kitty said.

"You work there to refine your taste. The competition is awful. They wouldn't do my Italian lamps show, they said I wasn't ready for a third promotion. I'd only put in six years. My doctor told me it was no wonder I couldn't conceive a child under that kind of pressure. It's been five weeks since I quit and I still haven't conceived."

Kitty didn't want to think about Helen's life choices right now; it was as if Fate had intervened when her assistant, Serge, buzzed her to say Judy Thaxter of *Gossip* was on 34. "Listen, Helena, " Kitty said, "we're having a small emergency here. Can I call you back?"

Though Helena hated manipulative people, she wanted to be in control of the conversation when she talked to Kitty again. So she unplugged her phone while she was having lunch. When she was finished she sat down at her new American pine and formica desk—which quoted from the fifties with its ameba-shaped top with the ameba-shaped holes in it—plugged the phone back in, and dialed Kitty's private number before Kitty could call her.

"I was just going to call you," Kitty said.

"That's good, then you have a minute. I need your advice." Helena drew the profile of a pregnant woman on the white pad in front of her. "Ever since I quit my job I've been waking up feeling blank in the morning," she said.

"I feel numb sometimes," Kitty said, "but never blank."

"Actually I don't feel blank, it's the day that feels blank. I feel as if someone turned the light off, and I can't tell where I am."

"You need a job," Kitty said.

"I need to be pregnant." Helena flushed with the strain of admitting this particular half-wish into speech. She drew a light bulb inside the pregnant woman so its rays filled her belly.

"Take it easy," Kitty said patiently. "You'll get pregnant when you're ready."

"How could I be more ready? I've set aside the next nine months. If anything, I'm probably trying too hard."

"What do you mean by trying too hard?" Kitty said.

Helena's face was burning. "During sex. Pulling, squeezing. It would be a laugh if I turned out to be sterile. Meanwhile Billy Greenburg is maneuvering his way toward curator of twentieth-century design."

Kitty said, "Why don't you go into business for yourself. You're too ambitious to be sitting around waiting."

Although she liked the idea of accomplishing something noticeable, Helena considered ambition to be unfeminine. "I'm not ambitious," she said. "My ambition is to be a mother before I'm thirty-five."

Kitty said, "I'm going to make my first million before I have my first baby."

"Don't ask me for advice if you're too old to get your muscle tone back." Helena wrote on her pad, FLAB, FLAB, FLAB. Then she made the Fs into Bs and used dots to make all the Bs into sets of breasts. "I have thought about doing some interior design jobs while I'm waiting," she said. "I don't think so, though. Being responsible for what kind of sheets your clients sleep on, and what utensils they use—

that's very intimate contact to have with someone you wouldn't have to know under ordinary circumstances."

Kitty said, "Excuse me for a just a minute, okay?" and put Helena on hold. Helena thought about spoons, waiting for Kitty to come back on the line. "That was the fish cook. There are no redfish to blacken. I told him to blacken some bluefish. Why not? It will be our invention," she said. "The customers will eat it up. I love to think about all the digestive systems in this city turning my work into protoplasm every day. I really get off on being influential."

Helena said, "If I went into business for myself I'd never make money. I don't know how to dun people."

"Dunning is one of my favorite chores," Kitty said.

To take advice, Helena reflected, wasn't at all as gratifying as to give it. "Aren't you afraid you're too successful for any man to want to marry you?" she said.

"Of course not. Success is an aphrodisiac."

"John married me because I was a lady."

"I'm never more ladylike than when I'm asking for money. I call up in my sweetest voice and I say, 'Hi, I hate to bother you, but you must have forgotten to pay your bill.' I always act as if they're in the right. Serge calls me Miss Mealymouth, but I'm making them feel ashamed of themselves."

"Don't they tell you hard-luck stories? I'd be embarrassed to listen to them."

"Think of it as a fox hunt. The idea is to corner the fox, not to feel sorry for him. There wouldn't be any fox hunts in the first place if they didn't go around raiding chicken coops."

"If I thought of my clients as foxes raiding my chicken coops I wouldn't want to do a good job for them."

"Use that. That's a great idea. I had a psychiatrist once

who used that on me. Tell them you can't feel the sympathy you need to work with them unless they pay you. Make them pay you in steps. That's perfect. God, I wish I were in the art business."

"It is good, isn't it?" Helena turned to a new page in her pad and drew a barbed-wire fence. The crisscrossed pencil lines made her feel queasy. "The truth is," she said, "John's the one who wants the baby more than I do. He tells me parents have put themselves in touch with the chain of life. He got that from a book he's publishing about parenthood. It's the only book on his whole fall list he's interested in. He's fifty-two. I think he needs to be a father. I'll look pretty selfish if I refuse him."

"Don't refuse him, just don't put all your eggs in one basket."

"Hoho," Helena said. "Is that some kind of farm girl pun?"

Kitty said, "Damn. I'll have to call you back."

Kitty talked first to a pasta maker who wanted her to try his new lettuce linguine (with natural opium) instead of the spinach fettucini she'd ordered from him; then to a mycologist who claimed he'd just discovered—and wanted to market—an American wild mushroom that tasted like black truffles; then to a rye bread baker whose delivery boy was on strike; then she yelled at Serge for letting her messages pile up. Then she felt bad about yelling at Serge.

"Let me tell you about the party," she started out, when she finally got back to Helena a half hour later. "I'm having linguine with chocolate sauce, pale green salad, semolina bread, champagne and raspberries. We've just started importing madeleines from France. Isn't that what Proust ate? I'm going to have madeleines for Judy."

"Who's Judy?"

"Judy Thaxter, the *Gossip* reporter. The waiters will all have dark hair, parted in the middle, and moustaches. I'm having forty or fifty people. I haven't told anyone but you about *Gossip* coming."

"You'd better. You don't want anyone being indiscreet without knowing it."

"Do you think I'm letting myself in for trouble?"

"If I were you I'd skip the hairdos on the waiters. It will look too much like musical comedy." Helena was silent for a good fifteen seconds. "You know the reporter will have something to say about those terrible photographs in your bathroom," she said. "I've never understood why you have them there."

Kitty reminded herself she liked Helena for her good taste. "All my beautiful copulators?" she said. "They're just people indulging their appetites."

"Are you going to leave your animal trophies up in the kitchen?"

So the trophies were vulgar, too. "I think they add warmth to the room," Kitty said. "Besides, if I take them off the walls one of my friends will tell her she ought to see them. Then I'll have to say they're out being cleaned. I just hope she doesn't ask any embarrassing questions."

"What would embarrass you?"

Kitty lowered her voice as if someone might overhear. "I was arrested once for shoplifting."

"But every kid shoplifts. I stole a bag of Tootsie Rolls from a candy store when I was ten. I was visiting with a girl friend who lived in a kind of slum neighborhood."

"I was seventeen. I put an angora sweater on under my blouse in Barton's department store. It was easy to spot me with the blue fuzz all over my black skirt. My father let me spend a night in jail to teach me a lesson. That was when I realized I'd never have fluffy things in my life if I didn't get out of Longpond, Ohio."

"I think that's a good story."

"Don't tell anyone, okay? I'd die if anybody knew my father was so mean to me."

"Maybe it's lucky your father's dead."

"My father's not dead."

"I thought you told me he died when you were in high school."

"Do you think I can get away with making up my childhood?" Kitty said.

"Sure. I guess so. As long as it's a good, plausible story and you stick to it, why would the reporter care if it's true or not?"

"I'll say my mother was French, and she trained me from childhood to distinguish tastes. She had an herb garden outside the kitchen and was especially fond of tarragon. It was in her salads that I first tasted tarragon vinegar. My palate was highly developed before I knew what a palate was. Compared to my mother's cooking, all the food I ate away from home tasted like lima beans and marshmallows.

"Every August we went out on cool mornings and picked blueberries on a sand hill near the farm. We picked until we were stained scarlet with the juice and we'd filled a kettle and five saucepans. No matter how many blueberries we picked there were always more, and to me each was a jewel. They fell into the pans with such voluptuous little thuds. I was a speedy picker. Full saucepans meant blueberry muffins, blueberry pancakes, blueberry pie, blueberry ice cream. You don't know what it's like to bite into a moist blueberry in the middle of a sweet, warm muffin if you haven't had my mother's blueberry muffins. For my twelfth birthday my mother baked a blueberry cake with custard sauce that moved me so deeply I knew I wanted to share her cooking with the world when I grew up. Then when I was eighteen she died of tuberculosis."

"Then she's the one who's dead," Helena said. "But who was that sweet, white-haired woman I met in New York last fall, the one with the steel-rimmed glasses and the bun on top of her head? Wasn't that your mother?"

"Maybe I could say she stopped cooking after an oven blew up in her face."

"Why don't you just say you can't remember your childhood."

"Can I put you on hold for a minute?" Kitty said. "Speaking of buns, there's something I have to tell the pastry chef."

Helena leafed through the new *Insides and Outsides,* holding the receiver between ear and shoulder. She liked the way glass bricks softened light, even though glass brick walls were becoming a cliché. She loved Chinese lacquer screens. Wooden houses that were shaped like igloos looked awful, no matter how functional they were. She wished her other line would ring so she'd be unavailable when Kitty finished her interminable conversation. How much could she have to say about buns?

"Sorry," Kitty said, getting back on the line. "You're terrific to be helping me with this party. Weren't you about to say something?"

Helena loved Kitty for appreciating her. "I was going to ask what the party's celebrating," she said.

"That's a good question."

"Don't you think it's better to have a party in honor of someone or something? My mother always did. She used to say it gave the guests a stake in making the party a success."

"Well, naturally there's a purpose," Kitty said. "It's Giorgio."

"Not you, too."

"Why not? Alexandra doesn't want him."

"She loves to talk about how he wants her. Why don't you wait until she drops him?"

"I'll just be giving the situation a slight push," Kitty said. "I think Giorgio really likes me but he's hung up on Alexandra because she gives him such a hard time. Let's see what happens when the three of us are in a room together."

Helena said, "I thought you were interested in Anthony Foot."

"I'm not," Kitty said.

"Uh huh." Helena didn't know whose friend she was supposed to be. She liked Alexandra at least as much as she liked Kitty—but probably Kitty was right about the Giorgio situation. In any case, she was the one who was asking for advice. "You don't want the party to be for Giorgio," Helena said, "or all the girls will be after him. If it's for Alexandra, he'll be after her. Anyway, a party for Alexandra would be cynical." As she preferred in situations where her loyalties were divided, she was managing to be loyal to everybody at the same time.

"I have the perfect idea," Kitty said. "The party will be for you."

"For me?" Helena's mood brightened instantly; she began to think about her guest list. "Why for me?" she said.

"To launch your design business. Everyone there will be a potential client."

"It's a great idea," Helena said, "but I don't know if I'm

going to launch a design business. What if I decide to write a book instead?"

"Then you'd be the one who'd have to do the explaining," Kitty said. "Why don't you want to have a baby?"

Helena didn't like indecisiveness. It was turning her against the baby before she'd even conceived it. "I do want to have a baby," she said. "It's just that I'm perfectly happy without one. I'm afraid if my husband has a baby he might stop babying me. Please don't tell him I said that."

"Not if you don't tell Alexandra about Giorgio and me."

"Anyway, a baby's an enormous commitment. What if I fell in love with someone else? What if John left me?" Helena felt queasy again. "I'd better get off the phone," she said. "I think I'm going to vomit."

"Maybe you're pregnant," Kitty said.

Helena hung up and lay down on her midnight-blue velvet Art Deco sofa. When she thought of being without her husband it was as if all the lamps and chairs she'd ever bought, and the comfortable rooms she'd arranged them in, had been torn from her, and she was on an island no bigger than her two feet, surrounded by empty space and totally defenseless. She preferred this awful fear of losing him to the prospect she had recently begun to entertain of no longer wanting him.

The fact was, he was not the same driven man she'd married. She told herself what she always did to put the question into perspective—that she'd never leave John unless, of course, Roger Rathbone wanted to marry her. She smiled as she imagined the amused blue eyes of the exquisite Roger Rathbone gazing into her eyes from an enormous movie screen. In less than a minute she was asleep.

•　•　•

Kitty flipped to this year's calendar at the back of her appointment book where every month she circled the date on which her period started. It wasn't due for another week and a half. She buzzed Serge. "Call the florist, sweetheart," she said, "and order five dozen tiger lilies for Saturday night. And tell the Host's Helpers to cancel the hairdos on the waiters."

THREE

Violet woke Kitty up at ten o'clock on the Sunday morning after her party. "I wanted to be the first to call," she said.

"You are the first," Kitty said.

"I've been up since six. Philip's fast asleep. I'm afraid to wake him up until he's had seven hours. We had an awful fight last night. I was so embarrassed—that reporter from *Gossip* was taking notes. The photographer got a picture. I wish I could remember what I said."

"Could you hold on while I get a robe?" Kitty said. You would think her satin sheets and her curly lamb fur throw would be enough to keep her warm. Violet picked up the *Times* crossword puzzle. What was a song title with three numbers in it that was forty-six letters long? It took up three lines in the puzzle, second letter *F*, seventeenth *L*, thirty-fifth *T.* "I think I had too much champagne," Kitty said, coming back to the phone. "My mouth feels as if something were sparkling in it all night."

"It was a great party," Violet said. "At least I think so. I kept wishing I weren't mad at Philip so I could enjoy myself."

Kitty yawned. "I'm only half awake," she said.

"Do you want me to call back?"

"What time is it?"

"Five minutes past ten. The thing is, I'm going out. We're having lunch with Philip's mother. You looked beautiful last night." Violet considered Kitty to be too sharp-featured, her chin too firm, her eyes too coldly green to be beautiful. Last night she had looked beautiful for Kitty.

"Did I?" Kitty said, warming to the conversation.

"Giorgio couldn't take his eyes off you. I felt so jealous. Philip was flirting with that bitch Rose LaFleur." As she pictured Philip smiling at Rose, telling her how much he liked the fey little books she wrote for children, Violet felt the same agitation that last night had caused her to grab a little piece of flesh at his waist through his pale blue oxford-cloth shirt and twist it until he slapped her wrist. "Sometimes I think Philip's just using me while he looks around for someone more romantic to fall in love with," she said tremulously.

"Was that what was wrong with you last night?" Kitty said. "You seemed a little out of control."

"I did? What do you mean?"

"You were following Philip around. I tried to talk to you and you motioned me away. Your teeth were clenched."

"I clench my teeth when I'm thinking. Did you hear our argument?"

"I couldn't help it. You were yelling at him."

"I wasn't yelling. I was snapping, maybe." Violet's left eyelid began to flutter. She hoped she wasn't going to need glasses. "What did you hear?" she said.

"You told him you didn't like the way he was looking at Alexandra and besides, if she let him make love to her she'd be disappointed."

"What?"

"You said, 'Don't show me up by fucking any of my friends. I always pretend you're a great lay.' "

"Who else heard?"

"Only the people on our side of the room. The ones who didn't walk away."

Kitty had no tact at all. "Was Lucio Bergonzi on our side of the room?"

"I don't remember. Why?"

"I was wondering if I ruined myself professionally, too. Before I got angry I gave Lucio twenty reasons why Star-Time should represent him."

"You don't handle opera stars, do you?"

"I think Lucio could be a movie-star opera star. That was my main point. Anyway, opera's going to get very big, soon."

"Opera already is very big," Kitty said.

"I wish I'd never gotten up this morning." Violet shifted her weight in the white wicker chaise, turning her back on the glamorous white gardenias going brown around the edges on the bedside table, and the mound of blankets with Philip under it in the middle of the bed. "I hope he's not still mad at me," she said.

Kitty said. "He's such a sweet man. If I had him I'd be nice to him."

It was easy to be a goody-goody about men when you

didn't happen to be dealing with one day in and day out. "He doesn't care if I'm nice as long as I'll have sex whenever he wants," Violet said.

"Really?"

"He's the one who's not nice to me. He flirts with other women. As soon as I started talking to Lucio he started cruising Rose. I saw him fill up her dinner plate for her."

"Don't you think he would have done the same for you if you'd been standing next to him in the food line?"

"That's not the point." Violet felt cranky all of a sudden. "I think couples should spend time with other people at parties. Otherwise why bother to go to a party?"

"Then what's the problem?"

"He doesn't love me, or he'd hate being separated from me. Which reminds me. Did you see Helena and John holding hands? If he's planning to leave her he's doing a good cover-up job."

"I never said he was planning to leave her." Kitty was talking very deliberately, as if she thought Violet had a zero attention span. "I said Rebecca was giving away her cat and all her old clothes. She told Aida she wants to get rid of the possessions in her life. It's Aida who thinks she's really making room for her boyfriend to move in. Aida's her cleaning lady, not her best friend. I don't always tell Aida the exact truth, either. I embroider a little so she'll brag about me to the other people she cleans for. Anyway, maybe Rebecca has another boyfriend besides John."

Violet said, "You'll have to tell me again why you don't think any of us should give Helena a hint."

"Don't you dare," Kitty said. "Helena's been handling it beautifully in her own way. Unconsciously. If she found out about the real situation through you, she'd feel as if she had to do something about it for your sake, even if she thought it was better not to."

The tie on Violet's bathrobe was constricting her breathing. She sat up and loosened it. "I know," she said. "Helena would rather die than have a fight in public."

"Fighting in public just isn't smart," Kitty said. "It doesn't have much charm, either."

In another ten minutes Violet could wake up Philip. He would tell her if she'd been charming or not last night. First she'd better put on mascara. "I should go now," she said, "and let you get some sleep."

"That's great, now that I'm awake. If I get up I'll have to start cleaning," Kitty said.

"Didn't all those cute waiters clean up? Did you notice they all had the same hairdo?"

"That was a mistake," Kitty said. "Tell me what else you noticed about Giorgio."

Violet loved romance, even though she didn't think of Giorgio—who was short and had an Italian accent and talked too much about fast cars and dry wines—as romantic. "He was looking at you, wherever you were, all night," she said.

"How about Alexandra? Did he look at her?"

"Well, he brought her, of course, but I didn't see them together after that. Alexandra spent half the time making eyes at Philip. Then when she saw he was hopelessly involved with Rose LaFleur, she went off to a corner with a man whose name was Sweet. Can that be right? He was big. Square shoulders, round head, tweed jacket, horn-rimmed glasses. He looked like you could lean on him."

"That's Henry Sweet, my best new customer," Kitty

said. "He runs the Sweet School of Human Possibility. Teaches people to love themselves. After every class he serves my health-food cakes and cookies."

"That reminds me," said Violet, who'd become agitated again at the mention of the word *love,* "how are those truffle muffins of yours after a week in the refrigerator? I thought I'd bring some to Philip's mother."

"They get better in the refrigerator," Kitty said. "Did Alexandra leave with Henry?"

"I think I left before she did. Why? Are you interested in Henry?"

"I'm interested in Giorgio."

Kitty got where she was by being single-minded. "Then I'm sure you'll get him," Violet said. "And I want to hear all about it, but it's about time to wake up Philip right now, and if I don't I'm going to bite all my nails off."

"Call me back," Kitty said.

Violet hung up so fast she forgot to ask Kitty if she knew a forty-six-letter song title with three numbers in it.

Kitty got out of bed. She was cold, her head felt heavy, and there was something she wanted to do. As she walked toward her dressing table to look at her unmade-up face in a kind light, a red stocking slid from the top of the mirror to the floor. Where was the dress she'd worn with it? Giorgio. Giorgo had got the dress half unzipped in the kitchen last night while she was washing champagne glasses. She'd let him cover her back with kisses. She shivered as she thought about it. He had a sweet tongue. She'd led him into the living room where Jamaican reggae was playing. Oh God, there was the dress, like a pool of blood on the white living room carpet where she'd slithered out of it. It had rug lint in its sequins. Giorgio's watch was on the coffee table; he'd placed it there before he'd kissed her lips. Her lips. She'd better call Alexandra.

"Hi, darling." Alexandra sounded slow, as if her mechanism hadn't been wound up for the day. "I was going to call you as soon as I finished meditating. I left Giorgio at your party last night. I had important things to say to Henry. I hope you didn't mind."

"You know I think Giorgio's divine," Kitty said.

"I just got off the phone with him. He said, 'Your friend Kitty, she's the perfect hostess. She knows how to make her guests feel at home.' "

"That was nice of him."

"Do you know what he meant? I think he was trying to make me jealous. Men are so transparent."

At least Alexandra hadn't slammed down the phone. Later on, someone would tell her that Giorgio wasn't hers to speak of in that proprietary manner anymore. Kitty felt relieved and changed the subject. "How did you like the linguine with chocolate sauce?" she said. A good food conversation could distract Alexandra even from thoughts of men.

"Was that what that was? It was wonderful, darling. I had three helpings. But what do you think about the color? Isn't it a little drab?"

"It's brown. The color of chocolate."

"I guess so. Maybe you should try it with sprinkles. Green pistachio nuts. They're full of protein. A little hard to digest, maybe."

"Did you like the madeleines?"

"Those cookies? Were those madeleines? Oh, thank God. I had the weirdest experience. You know, I've been reading Proust. I'm still on the first book, *Swann's Way*. Every time I put it down for a minute I forget where the thought began and I have to start again. Anyway, after my three helpings of linguine with chocolate sauce a waiter came up with a tray of shortbread and I took one. I didn't know they were madeleines. I took a bite, and I looked up at the waiter and he had a moustache and his hair was parted in the middle and he looked like Marcel Proust. Then I looked around and all the waiters looked like Marcel Proust. I almost fainted. I thought I was having thought materializations. I've had them before, and they're very exciting, but what scared me was I hadn't been thinking of Proust."

"It must have been the madeleines," Kitty said. She was going to make Serge pay for those waiters.

"Madeleines have got to be powerful," Alexandra said. "Proust was a genius. I had a long talk about him with Henry Sweet. Henry thinks Proust's asthma could have been cured nutritionally. But then, without his feverishness, would he have been so brilliant?"

Kitty said, "I thought you two might get along." She couldn't understand how Giorgio could be interested in her and Alexandra at the same time. "Did he take you home?"

"He came up for tea and we talked. He's very humble. He told me he doesn't know why he was chosen for his calling—he used to be pretty happy when he worked as a lawyer and sued people. So now he soothes people. His students are just like my listeners. They turn to us because they can't find any love in the world."

"I guess love is something Henry knows a lot about," Kitty said.

"If you're talking about what I think you're talking about I wouldn't know," said Alexandra. "I don't think he's interested in bodies. That's why he can be so focused."

Kitty had a sudden feeling Giorgio was trying to get her. For the moment she was sorry she hadn't installed call-waiting service at home. "I'd better go clean up," she said.

"I had a funny conversation with a woman named Judy Thaxter last night, if you want to hear," said Alexandra.

"Oh yeah? Tell me about it."

"She was asking a lot of questions about you. Is she a new friend of yours? Her slip was showing."

"I don't know yet. She's writing about me for *Gossip*. What did you tell her?" The possibility of disgrace in a national magazine flashed across Kitty's consciousness like a lightning bolt charging through a murky sky. If she weren't worrying about Giorgio, she thought, she'd be scared right now.

"*Gossip*, huh? What I told her will be great for *Gossip*," Alexandra said. "I said I thought you were a wonderful businesswoman because you really loved success and money."

"How did the subject come up?"

"I don't know. I thought it was just girl talk. We were standing in line outside the bathroom. Gordon Blair and two of his friends were inside doing coke. I don't think it's fair of people to do drugs in bathrooms at parties when other people want to do makeup, do you? I had to bang on the door three times before they opened up. There they were leaning against the mirror, smiling. Gordon had coke between his nostrils. His friend Alistair was putting a pillbox into his pocket. The least they could have done was to offer us a little something for making us wait. But Gordon is too glazed over to have any manners anymore. We used to be such good friends."

"How did Judy take all of this?"

"Oh, she didn't seem interested in the coke at all. She just wanted to know about the sex pictures in the bathroom."

"What did you tell her?"

"I said what I always say. 'Kitty thinks people should make friends with their passions.' She asked what your passions were. I said, 'Hunting, for one.' By the way, where were your animal trophies last night?"

"Out being cleaned," Kitty said.

"Good," said Alexandra. "That's what I told Judy."

Alexandra got off the phone with an uneasy feeling. As much as she tried it was hard for her to love Kitty's pushiness and her unscrupulous behavior concerning men. To make matters worse, she'd told Henry Sweet she would spend the day casting out anger from her life. Henry said it was anger that gave her hungers, and here she was definitely verging on anger. She pulled herself up cross-legged on her straight-backed chair, closed her eyes, and began to repeat a Sanskrit phrase over and over to herself as if to go into a trance. The thoughts she had, though she let them float in and out of her mind without holding on to them, nevertheless kept coming back. Kitty reminded her of her big sister Alice who used to steal her toys. Alice had broken the smiling head off her clown doll. Twenty minutes into the meditation Alexandra stopped and called Helena. "Hello, darling, are you all right today?" she said. Whenever she was feeling shaky Alexandra worried about her friends.

Helena said, "I'm throwing out my aluminum pots and

pans. John says there's a rumor aluminum causes Alzheimer's disease."

"Oh, no, darling, is that why I can't remember anything?"

"John thinks it's funny, but I don't want to take any chances when I might be pregnant soon."

"It's not funny," Alexandra said. "You don't want to have the first baby with Alzheimer's disease."

Helena said, "Who was that big man you were talking to last night? The one with the very bland face? I always wonder what's going on behind those bland faces."

"His name is Henry Sweet. He reminds me of a football player I went out with in college. Only Henry's a very spiritual man, very wise. Did you happen to notice where Giorgio was while I was talking to Henry?"

"Where you left him, I'm sure," Helena said.

"I guess I left him." Alexandra's voice came out flat. She wasn't certain whether feeling sorry for yourself was a case of casting out anger or drawing it to you. "Do you think Kitty is after him?" she said.

"I thought you didn't want him," said Helena. "Maybe if he was in love with Kitty he'd stop bothering you with those annoying phone calls."

"That's true," Alexandra said. "I don't have much in common with him. We don't have long, deep conversations the way I had with Henry Sweet last night. If only Henry needed a woman, he's a man I could inspire. But there's no way I can be Giorgio's inspiration—he doesn't do anything interesting enough. What I like best about him is his confidence, and I know if he were more spiritually developed he wouldn't be so confident."

"How can you tell the difference between confidence and inner peace?" Helena said.

"Before you can find inner peace you have to doubt everything. Giorgio doesn't doubt. Sure, he makes me feel secure when he tells me there's nothing to worry about, but that's not a good reason to fall in love." Alexandra took the snow globe with the little glass farm inside it from the big oak desk a beautiful hippie carpenter built for her ages ago. What was his name? Bert. She made it snow on the farm. "I still don't want Kitty going after him behind my back," she said.

Helena didn't say anything. There was nothing that made Alexandra more nervous than dead air, and Helena knew it. "Darling, are you there? Don't go unconscious on me. I need you," Alexandra said after forty-five seconds of silence. She heard the clang of an aluminum pot hitting the stove.

"If Kitty told you she was interested in Giorgio and asked your permission to go after him, would that be okay with you?" Helena said.

"Why can't she find her own man?"

"You sound upset. Maybe you really want him and you just think he's not your type," Helena said.

"I couldn't want him." Alexandra felt as if a big hole had opened in her stomach. "Can you hold on a minute," she said. She went to the kitchen and got a quart of frozen raspberry goat's milk yogurt from the freezer. She had five spoonfuls before she picked up the phone again. "Sorry," she said. "I had such a craving for food, it was like a panic. I haven't eaten since I got up."

"I hate to be left dangling in the middle of a conversation," Helena said. "Kitty does it, too. With her it's her other lines ringing. I think people should do one thing at a time."

"I could live on raspberry yogurt," Alexandra said. "What were you saying about Kitty and Giorgio?"

"I was just saying that since you don't want him, why not let Kitty have him?"

"So she *is* after him."

"I don't know. But so what if she is, since you're not?"

Alexandra was beginning to feel calmer now that she was eating. "You're probably right," she said. "It's the adult thing to do. I just want a man who'll call me three times a day." What she'd said made her throat burn and she spooned raspberry yogurt down to cool it.

"Did you talk to the reporter from *Gossip* last night?" Helena said.

"I just found out that's who she was. She asked a lot of questions about Kitty's love life. I'd be embarrassed to be that nosy."

"She caught me with a mouth full of chocolate sauce. I've been trying to get Kitty on the phone for the past half hour to talk about it." Helena yawned. "What are you doing this afternoon?" she said. "As soon as I can get off the phone I'm going for a long walk."

"I don't know. I'm very sad right now," said Alexandra with a grand sigh. "Probably because I'm trying to grow up." She looked down to see she'd finished a quart of yogurt, and she was still hungry.

Helena was sitting on the blue velvet sofa breaking up a sheet of stamps honoring the James brothers, Henry and William, when she finally got through to Kitty at noon. "I didn't want to wake you," she said testily. "Then your line was busy for an hour and a half."

"Violet called at ten," Kitty said. "Violet doesn't care

about waking people. I got to sleep at five. I can't get back to sleep because of my headache. Every time I hang up, the phone rings again."

Helena thought complaining about one's good fortune was the height of bad manners. You had to be incredibly selfish to expect to lord it over others and get sympathy at the same time. "If you don't want people to call and thank you for your party, just unplug your phone," she said.

Kitty said, "I'm expecting a call from Giorgio. He left his watch here. That must mean he wants to come back. At least unconsciously."

"He left his watch, huh? How did he happen to take his watch off?"

"Just the way you think," Kitty said.

"And are you in love?"

"I love his tongue."

Helena found the details of other people's sexual experiences to be mildly disgusting. She never told people what went on between her and John. After seven years of marriage, for an example, she had no feelings one way or the other about John's tongue. "His tongue," she said, folding the stamps in rows along their tops and bottoms, "I'll have to take a look the next time I see him."

"He makes love in Italian," Kitty said, as if that explained everything.

"That must be romantic." Helena didn't want to know what Giorgio said in Italian while he made love. John, in the throes of his passion, never talked at all. "Speaking of romance," she said, "did you see Gordon last night? Every time I turned around he was taking some good-looking man to the bathroom. Don't gay people have bars for that?"

Kitty said, "It's not romance, it's cocaine."

"Cocaine? That's the drug that makes people obnoxious. They go into bathrooms so other people won't see them sniffing it and that way everyone knows exactly what they're doing." Helena folded the stamps in rows along their sides. "No one's ever sniffed cocaine in my bathrooms. As a hostess you could have asked them to stop," she said.

"Gordon gave me half a gram for a present. I like it for sex."

Helena tore the stamps in vertical rows. "I was rattled enough before you started talking about sex, just from dialing your number over and over," she said. She tore the stamps off one by one and began inserting them in her beautiful flat Swedish stamp holder.

Kitty said, "I saw you having a long conversation with Larry Atwill."

"I like old men who wear those little string ties. They aren't pretending to be sophisticated. He said to me, 'You know, I know everything about meat—packing, shipping, distribution—that's my business, but I'm only beginning to learn about the beauty in life.' I told him I knew where to buy the most exquisite things in New York. I thought we were talking about furniture, but we were talking about Scarlett. He said Scarlett grew up poor, and now she wants to live on a Manhattan plantation. That's a challenge for a designer. You could do something great with indoor columns." Helena took *American Farms* off the late-sixties glass coffee table and put it in her lap. She wanted to have another look at the front views of the three plantations she'd looked at this morning. "I don't think it's right for women to marry men that much older than they are," she said. "I hope Scarlett is good to Larry. She has a very limp handshake."

"She's probably good in bed," Kitty said.

"I'm talking about character. I think your handshake says everything about your character."

Kitty said, "She kissed me on both cheeks."

"That's a terrible affectation for an American. Americans do it to show how worldly they are. They seem to think if you're worldly enough you can actually turn French," Helena said. "On the other hand I like it as a greeting. It's absolutely clear that you're making a gesture, not giving affection."

Kitty said, "Did you get the job?"

"I don't make deals at parties. I don't think anyone should be asking you to dance while you're negotiating," Helena said. "I actually lose my balance when I try to talk business standing up."

"I never lose my balance when I'm talking business," Kitty said. "How did you leave it with him?"

"We left it open," Helena said. "We were having supper together, discussing it on the window seat, when that photographer from *Gossip* snapped our picture. I wish he'd taken a picture of John and me. Next thing I knew the reporter was asking me questions."

"Judy Thaxter."

"Judy Thaxter. That's the real reason I called." Helena felt uncomfortable about her conversation with Judy Thaxter without knowing why, exactly. "She was very persistent. She wanted to know what made you so driven."

"Driven? Is that what she's going to say about me? I'd better have a talk with her," Kitty said.

Helena flipped through the book in her lap. It opened to an Ohio dairy farm. She tried to picture Kitty as a cute little girl wandering around the farm. Hadn't she said she had a special feeling for cows? "I told Judy as far as I knew you'd

always been as wonderful as you are now," Helena said.
"And you are wonderful, to have given that party for me."
Having secured every loose end she could think of for the
day she hung up and asked John to go with her to Central
Park.

Kitty wished she had someone to talk to. A woman took a
risk trusting other women with her secrets—that is, if she
could get them to pay attention at all. Men were much more
solid as confidants—but they were usually interested for
sexual reasons.

Giorgio would have been the perfect person to discuss
her problem with, except that her problem this morning was
Giorgio. What if he'd only desired her last night because he
hadn't had her before. That was a masochistic idea, and yet
she entertained it. Giorgio was a man of the world. If he
wanted to please a woman he'd made love to the night before he knew enough to call her early the next day. Her
head throbbed. She missed her office with its ringing
phones where she was always too busy to worry about anyone's feelings. Work was easy compared to love. If only she
didn't love sex so much she'd be celibate.

She tried to think of Giorgio as if last night had never
happened. Immediately she remembered the way his body
had entered hers. She tried concentrating on his faults—his
thinning hair, his way of changing the subject before you'd
had your fill of it—until she realized this was another excuse to think about him.

She walked from her bed to the window and looked out at
the garden where daffodils were booming. An ivy-covered
trellis partially blocked her view of her downstairs neighbors, two cheerful lesbians, who were strolling and holding

hands. Their old black poodle, which they kept unclipped, waddled behind them yipping like a puppy. Filled with melancholy, Kitty dialed Violet's number.

Kitty was on the white sofa reading a pasta cookbook and her phone machine was answering when Violet returned her call. "Hello, this is five five five, one one six one" she heard her own voice say. "Please leave a message when you hear the beep. Meow."

She resisted her impulse to pick up the phone and interrupt Violet's message. Your friends would suspect your sincerity if they knew you were screening their calls. Instead she went into the kitchen, poured herself a champagne glass full of San Pellegrino—which she'd told Giorgio last night she considered to be the champagne of bottled waters—and called Violet on her bedside phone.

"You were home all along," Violet said.

Kitty said, "Thanks for calling me back."

"Were you home?"

"I was in the bath. The phone's been ringing all day. Giorgio didn't get through until an hour ago. I was beginning to think he'd been mugged."

"You take lots of baths," Violet said, as if she never screened calls with her machine. In fact, Kitty had been shocked at Violet's one night when she'd let her guests overhear her callers leaving their messages. In Kitty's opinion callers had the right to be informed when they were playing for an audience. "When did you add the 'Meow'?" Violet said.

"Do you like it? I don't want to say my name anymore. There are too many obscene callers around."

"Don't you think animal noises might turn them on?"

"Not at all," Kitty said. "Animal noises are actually

calming. Is this a bad time for you to talk? It's not too good for me because Giorgio's going to be here in a half hour."

"I'm just feeling bratty. Philip says I was awful last night because I'm a person of contrasts. He says when I'm wonderful he loves me all the more because I'm awful sometimes."

"If I were you I'd hold on to him," Kitty said.

"He's worried because I'm going to L.A. in two weeks to help Glenda Crane come out of retirement," Violet said. "Sometimes I think Philip's a little wishy-washy."

"Giorgio's very firm in his way." Kitty felt a rush of warmth in her upper abdomen as she thought about the firmness of Giorgio. "He said last night he thinks it's no good to live alone. Then he said he wanted me to have a dog," she said.

"That's great," Violet said. "That's practically saying he wants you to have his baby. Why don't you get a pale Afghan hound to match your hair. They're supposed to be stupid, but so what? You don't need a smart dog to catch a man."

"I'll bet Giorgio would be a wonderful father. He's so warm." Kitty turned, looked over her shoulder and winked at herself across the room in the dressing table mirror. "And speaking of Giorgio," she said, "I have to start getting ready for him right now."

Violet said, "On your message you said you were having a problem with him."

"I did?" Kitty said. "That must have been this morning, when I still had hours to wait before I could see him again."

"Actually I called you to ask a question," Violet said. "What's a forty-six-letter song title with three numbers in it? The second letter is *F*, the tenth and eleventh are *L*, seventeenth *L*, twenty-fourth *Y*, thirty-fifth *T*, last letter *E*."

"'I Found a Million-Dollar Baby in a Five-and-Ten-Cent Store,'" Kitty said.

"I should have known that," said Violet. "It's one of my favorite song titles. It makes me think there's hope for me."

Kitty said, "You probably think that song is about a poor girl who gets discovered behind the notions counter by a man who thinks she's worth a million dollars. Well, it's not. It was actually written about Barbara Hutton, the Woolworth heiress. No smart woman gets discovered behind the notions counter unless she wants to be known for waiting on people."

FOUR

Violet stood at the window of her glamorous room at the Beverly Spa, noticing how gawky the palm trees were. "I think palm trees are a mistake in a city that wants to be taken seriously," Roger Rathbone had said to her not half an hour ago. In her hand she held the empty, neatly folded Between the Acts cigar packet Roger had given her on the plane. "This is my brand," he had said, as if he were trusting her with a secret. At the time she had found the gesture charming and romantic, suffused as it was with the overheated aura of Roger's physical presence. Now as she examined the packet in the white light of the late-afternoon California sun she thought of Philip for the first time since she'd left home.

Normally on a Sunday afternoon like this she and Philip would be having an early dinner and going to a movie, possibly one with Roger Rathbone in it. Philip was staying at her apartment while she was away, to look after things. He was too sweet to smoke cigars, and she was glad. She hated the smell of cigar smoke. She didn't like the name Between the Acts much, either. It seemed like an ironic comment on the nature of the relationship she and Roger might develop. She decided not to tell anyone about the packet, at least until she saw how things progressed. For the time being she put it in a drawer underneath a pile of underpants and the blue plastic case with her diaphragm in it.

Then she shut the blinds, turned on the TV picture without sound, put her feet up on the deep-rose quilted satin spread on her king-size bed and leaned back against the deep-rose quilted satin headboard. Feeling, at last, the way she liked to feel in a hotel, like a woman who got taken care of, she dialed the operator.

She'd promised herself not to call a girl friend on this trip unless she absolutely had to. She had to already.

No one answered at Helena's.

Kitty picked up the receiver on the sixth ring. "Did I get you out of the bath?" Violet said.

"You got me out of the kitchen," said Kitty. "Giorgio's here cooking osso buco the way his mother makes it."

"Oh, God, I got the time change backwards." Violet heaved a sigh and breathed in the sweet stale smell of tired tea roses. She hoped she hadn't overdone it when she'd sprayed herself with perfume on the plane. "I'm calling long-distance. Can you talk to me?" she said.

"If I talk to you, who's going to tell Giorgio what a good cook he is?" Kitty said.

"You're the only one I can tell this story to," Violet said. "I just picked up a movie star."

"Anyone I know?"

If Kitty weren't so acquisitive about men, Violet would
have called her first. "Roger Rathbone," she said, making
her voice as flat as she could.

"Oh, yeah?"

"He was sitting behind me on the plane. I noticed him
when he got up to go to the men's room. I could tell he was
someone by the way he moved his shoulders. Aggressive
but very casual. So on his way back I smiled at him. His
smile must be what got him into movies. He asked me if I
had a light."

"Englishmen are much more civilized than Americans,
even when they're like Roger," Kitty said.

Violet said, "You shouldn't believe everything you read.
He was very sweet. He told me he was uncomfortable with
strangers, but I didn't seem strange to him. He chain-
smoked baby cigars. Normally I wouldn't talk to strangers,
either, but when I'm traveling I feel the same way I feel at a
party—we all have something in common, so we're not
really strangers. Especially when I'm in first class."

"How about the guy you picked up in that bookstore in
the Village?"

Kitty would do better with people, men included, if she'd
learn to let things go by. "You mean Matthew," Violet said.
"That was different. He looked just like my brother Eddie. I
was in bed with him before I knew what I was doing."

"Roger buys caviar from me when he's in town," Kitty
said. "He calls me up at odd hours and wants it delivered to
his hotel room."

"Did he ever make a pass at you?"

"Not physically. Once he asked if I would deliver his
caviar myself. He was very insistent. I couldn't tell if it was
sexual desire or paranoia. In any case I don't make deliv-
eries. I sent a bonded messenger."

"His looks don't turn me on particularly," Violet said, "but I like the heat that comes off his body. I felt it as soon as he sat down next to me." She pulled one end of the bedspread around her and huddled into it.

"Was he drinking?"

"He doesn't drink anymore. He does a little coke when he needs a lift." Violet imagined doing a little coke with Roger, possibly after dinner tonight in his room. "I think he'd be a good client for Star-Time," she said. "We could rehabilitate his image. I started my pitch on the plane. I told him a story my mother told me, about how sometimes stars get tarnished, and on Christmas Eve Santa sends his helpers out to polish them."

"You didn't."

"Don't worry, it was perfectly appropriate since we were flying, too. I said Freddy used to say we ought to change our name to Santa's Helpers."

"What did Roger say?"

"I'm not sure he got my point. He said he knows a man who claims the earth and everything on it was made up by a giant computer in the sky. The computer is real; we're figments of its imagination. He said the man has proof. He invited me to dinner tonight."

"Take my advice and don't mix business with pleasure," Kitty said.

"That's my rule, too," said Violet, who couldn't help wondering if Kitty was jealous, "but I think it can be waived in the case of movie stars."

"Movie stars *are* your business," Kitty said.

"I don't like blonds, anyway," Violet said, holding up in front of her eyes a ringlet of her own, carrot-colored hair. "Don't let me keep you from lover boy's lasagna."

"I'll call you if it's not too late when he leaves," Kitty said, "though frankly I hope it will be."

When Violet got back from her evening with Roger Rathbone it was 11:30 by her clock. She had to talk to somebody, so she called Alexandra who always said she got her most positive energy late at night. Alexandra might be too man-crazy to be trusted, but at least she'd be awake.

"Who's that?" Alexandra said, picking up the phone on the first ring as if she'd been dreaming about an intruder.

"I woke you up," Violet said. "There's no right time to call New York from here, not if you want to go out to dinner, too."

"I was just writing something for my radio audience," Alexandra said. "It's about friendship. It was making me so depressed I blanked out. Do you mind if I read it to you, darling?"

"It's not going to depress me is it?" Violet took a bite out of the rose-shaped white chocolate the chambermaid had left on her pillow and sat down on the bed. "I'm calling from the West Coast," she said.

"It starts like this," Alexandra said. " 'We all know about friendship. One definition of a friend is someone who wouldn't steal your man. But it's never that clear-cut, is it, darlings? Has a friend ever stolen a man from you? Maybe he wasn't someone you wanted to marry, but now he doesn't even call you anymore.

" 'You start having visions about all the things he must be doing for her—reserving romantic tables at fabulous restaurants, sending her flowers that look like his sex organs, planning a trip to Rio where you've always wanted to go with the man you love. Rio, darlings. Blame it on the Bossa Nova.

" 'You'd like to kill your friend but you're very polite. You remember how, just two weeks before she did it, you told her you wanted to get rid of this guy. Darlings, never tell a friend you want to get rid of a guy, unless you're actually engaged to somebody else.'

"That's it, that's the truth about friendship, isn't it?"

Violet said, "It sounds like you really miss Giorgio."

"It's not that I miss him," Alexandra said. "I've just been obsessing about her having him, that's all. Now tell me, my darling, what are you doing up at this hour?"

"I told you," Violet said, "I'm in Los Angeles. I just got back from dinner with Roger Rathbone. I got a message Philip called while I was out. Roger said he could tell from the way I looked at him that I was going to be important in his life."

"Was it before or after he made a pass at you?"

Violet wished Alexandra would let her tell her own story. "You mean you know him," she said.

"I used to."

"I knew it. Did you go to bed with him?"

"Five times, one weekend in 1971. He was a gorgeous young man." Alexandra sighed. "He was like a burning torch. But he had too much negative energy charging around inside him. I was afraid I'd be consumed."

"I think he'd be a great client for Star-Time. I'm going to call Freddy about him in the morning." The fact that Alexandra had already had Roger made him seem desirable to Violet. Desire made her look on Alexandra, with her radio voice and her sweet rosebud mouth, as a possible betrayer. "He's different now, in any case," she said.

"Actors are all the same," said Alexandra.

Violet hated to be told anyone else had privileged information. "He looks at you as if this is all a big joke," she said. "I like that kind of man. The woman who marries him will have a very exciting life."

"Did he take you to a fabulous restaurant?"

"He took me to his house in Malibu. He wanted to drive to get the flight out of his mind. He doesn't like feeling that someone else is at the controls. We ate at a diner on the way. He said he likes diners because they're full of ordinary people and he can forget he's so famous. Then five or six of the ordinary people asked him for his autograph. One was a very pretty girl, and if you think that was easy to take, it wasn't. I'm used to being the one who gets noticed." Violet contemplated the long, pale fingers of her ringless left hand. "Roger told me I was pretty enough to be in the movies," she said.

"You don't even have to be pretty to be in the movies," Alexandra said.

"I wouldn't want to be in the movies if I couldn't be the star, would you?"

Alexandra sighed. "They told me I had star quality, but I wasn't photogenic. It has to do with the planes in your face."

"I'd love to have a screen test," Violet said. She was thinking about certain photographs in which everyone said she looked gorgeous. "I guess they want to know whether you're an actress before they give it to you."

"So what happened with Roger?" Alexandra said.

"Nothing, really. We went to his house. He'd left his coke at the hotel. We sat on the patio and watched the waves come in. He built a fire. Even though he's big, he looked frail lifting the logs. He has practically no furniture. Just a lot of pillows with butterflies on them."

"Moths to a flame," Alexandra said.

"You know what he said to me? He said, 'This is the home I deserve. An empty house in Malibu, far from civilization, where the neighbors roast suckling pigs in the sand and the twinkling stars and lapping waves will drive you mad.' He said, 'I don't deserve a home. I use my homelessness to get passion into my performances.' I wasn't sure what he meant. He doesn't even live there you know. He sublets it out."

"He meant he thinks feeling sorry for himself is good for his art," Alexandra said.

"Is it?"

"Definitely not, but some actors believe it is."

"I felt really stupid. I said, 'Cheer up. Things will get better.'

"He said, 'You're sweet, but if you don't mind, I don't want to cheer up right now.'

"I've only worked with actors, I've never been so close to one. They think about themselves all the time just like women, don't they?"

"You mean he really didn't make a pass at you?"

Violet was afraid she'd reawakened Alexandra's interest in Roger. "After he said I was going to be important in his life he kissed my hand. It was the right thing to do. Rita may say sex should be as natural as waking up with the sun in the morning, but I don't think it's the same thing."

"Rita?"

"My daughter."

"That Rita. It's been so long since her name came up."

"I don't talk about her because she's away at school," Violet said. "That's where she should be at fourteen. That's what I was saying. If I were her age I might feel the way she does about sex. But I'm a different generation, even though

I had her when I was very young. I still think a man should court a woman. Especially in a case like this when nobody's introduced us. Kissing my hand was a way of saying he respected me. In fact, he didn't really turn me on until he didn't make a pass at me."

"Henry calls me every day to find out about the state of my mental health," Alexandra said. "But I don't think he's courting me. I think he wants to be a guest on my radio show."

Though she didn't understand the appeal of Giorgio, Violet thought Henry made Giorgio look like Clark Gable. In fact, the mention of Henry reminded her she was phoning long-distance. "There's a good movie on tonight," she said. "The one where Elizabeth Taylor talks about cannibalism and Montgomery Clift's name is Sebastian."

"Here it's three o'clock in the morning," Alexandra said.

Violet said, "I'd better call Philip."

"Fitzgerald said, 'In a real dark night of the soul it is always three o'clock in the morning,' " Alexandra said, "but I feel safe and protected at this hour because everyone else is asleep. My mind can expand and there's no one to get in the way. I wish I didn't want to cry right now."

"I wouldn't spend too much time with Fitzgerald if I were you," Violet said.

Violet's first call to Helena occurred the next morning after she'd showered, ordered breakfast and got the first call of the day from Freddy, and while she was still naked. It was about room service. "How do I tip room service?" she said. "Do I have to give them cash?"

"Not unless you're in an Iron Curtain country," Helena said.

"I'm in Los Angeles. Didn't I tell you I was going?"

"There it's okay to put fifteen percent on the bill, just like New York."

"What about the bellman? I gave him fifty cents a bag. Was that enough?"

"I would have given him a dollar. But it doesn't matter. You're not going to have to depend on him for anything."

"I'm sure fifty cents was enough." Violet liked to think she was generous to a fault. "Otherwise he wouldn't have smiled at me."

"Unless you smiled at him first."

"How am I supposed to know what to do?" Violet said in a shrill voice. "I never travel on my own. It's two years since I've been out of the same city as Philip."

"Don't worry. You can tip him again if he takes your bags down."

"And what about the cabdriver? How do I know he's taking me the quickest way? I couldn't ask Glenda Crane directions to her house. She's eighty years old and she used to be on the star tour. She thinks everybody knows where she lives."

"You know what to do. Make it clear to the driver you have business in town. Promise to call for him again if he's good. Act confident."

"I feel about as confident as a half grapefruit with all its membranes cut." Violet blew her nose, which was running. "And how about the pool boy. Do I tip the pool boy? If he gives me a towel? All the towels are pink here. And the sheets."

Helena said, "Is something wrong?"

"I'm in a panic, that's all. When I called Philip last night he was mad at me. It was after three in the morning, his time. I suppose he expected to hear from me as soon as I checked in, but he didn't say so. How was I to know?"

"I always miss John at six-thirty, when he usually gets home. The moment I realize he's not getting home that night, or not until late, I get a little sinking feeling."

"Maybe that's what Philip had," Violet said, but it was too upsetting to imagine Philip sinking because of her. "Anyway," she said, cheering up, "there's no time I usually get home on Sunday. I usually don't go out. And I couldn't call Philip because I was having dinner with Roger Rathbone."

"Roger Rathbone." Helena sounded interested at last. "He's very attractive."

At the same time that it was satisfying to know a movie star more intimately than other people did, it wasn't fully satisfying when all your friends had their own opinions about him. "He'd make a great client for Star-Time," Violet said. "But I couldn't tell Philip that at three o'clock in the morning."

"Pink is wonderful for your complexion," Helena said.

"What?"

"I was thinking about the pink towels and sheets. It must be wonderful with your red hair."

"There's no one here to notice," Violet said.

Helena said, "Will you introduce me to Roger Rathbone?"

"He has a suite just the other end of the hall. I wish I were there right now." Violet went to the window, whose blind was open on a gray morning. If a passerby happened to look up he would see her, tall, high-breasted and naked, watching him. But there were no passersby in the field she faced.

"Be serious," Helena said. "You don't want to get involved with a movie star."

"Why not?"

"Use a little self-control, Violet."

"I don't have any self-control," Violet said. "I just want to have a good time." Someone was putting up the pink-and-white poolside umbrellas in the distance. Otherwise nothing at all was happening outside. Violet went back to bed.

"Don't you have a good time with Philip?" Helena said sweetly.

"We fight so much. I think we must be incompatible."

"That could be," said Helena.

There was a soft knock on Violet's door. "I was hoping you'd give me an argument," she said, but she was actually glad that now there wasn't time. If she was going to get upset about Philip, she might as well be at home. "Room service is here," she said. "I have to put on my bathrobe so he doesn't think I want him to come in and rape me. Not that I'd go visit a neighbor at home wearing just a bathrobe. I don't know why it's all right to let perfect strangers see me in my nightclothes just as long as they're servants."

Violet hung up, put on her robe and opened the door to a stout, smiling, middle-aged Mexican-American in a white cotton waiter's jacket. On the food cart he pushed before him, plates and cutlery gently rattling, was a white vase with a single pink rose in it. Behind him in the otherwise empty hall, also pink, lolled Roger Rathbone—if *loll* was the right word for someone who seemed to be leaning lazily against a wall yet was also looking someone else up and down with intense concentration. The utter rudeness of it! Violet imagined he could see right through her robe to her naked, blushing body. Before she'd decided how to respond, the infuriating man smiled as if she'd said something terribly amusing, disengaged himself from the wall and strolled away, leaving her very hungry for breakfast.

• • •

Helena felt awful when she hung up. All she really wanted in life was for John to be as committed to success as she'd thought he was when she'd married him, so she could conceive his child without worrying about whether she'd always love him or not. Roger Rathbone was a harmless fantasy who helped her fall asleep sometimes. Now her best friend was flirting with him. She was as desperate as if Violet had destroyed her last hope. She called Alexandra at once. "Have you talked to Violet lately?" she said.

"Early this morning. I was asleep."

"I think she's making a mistake. Don't you?"

"You mean Roger? She says she wants him for a client."

Sometimes Alexandra talked like a fool. "I'm not as experienced as you single girls, and even I don't believe that," Helena said.

"Roger's not a mistake in any case," Alexandra said. "I know him very well. He's like a really rich, flourless chocolate cake. You eat too much before you know it, and then you get sick."

"You mean he's too good?"

"Not really. Just too much."

"I don't understand how that's possible," said Helena, who rarely ate chocolate, smoked a cigarette once a week and only drank at parties. "Why not take him in small doses?"

"He's not like that, believe me," Alexandra said.

Helena had the same kind of tight feeling in her chest that she got when she saw Roger Rathbone kiss a woman on screen. "I think you ought to talk to her," she said.

"Darling, I think you're overreacting," said Alexandra. "You don't even like Philip."

"I do like him. She just talks about him too much. Roger sounds as if he'd really give her something to complain about. Then she'll never get off the phone."

"So it's yourself you're worried about."

"I don't know." Helena hunched her shoulders and pressed her elbows to her sides. She felt hemmed in. "Maybe you could remind her," she said, "of her obligations to the public relations profession."

"You're probably not getting enough physical exercise."

"Violet's problems aren't going to clear up if I take a walk."

"There's no point saying anything to Violet," Alexandra said. "She's like you. She likes to give advice, not take it."

Alexandra loved her friends; they were the family she wished she'd had when she'd had a family. Even so, a conversation with one of them could knot up her whole digestive system, whose many convoluted passageways couldn't be more tangled than the lives of everyone she knew. She ate three stalks of celery and a huge organic carrot. Then she went into her bedroom and lay down on her bed, and though she didn't want to talk to her, she called Kitty. "Have you talked to Violet lately?" she said.

"It's wonderful, isn't it?" Kitty said. "All she has to do is get on a plane and movie stars fall all over her."

Apparently now that Kitty had chosen—or rather stolen—a man for herself, she resented the idea that other women were still free to make a choice. "Don't be jealous," Alexandra said.

"I was being appreciative," said Kitty. "I wouldn't go near Roger Rathbone. Too undisciplined. I like men you can reason with."

"Like Giorgio? Giorgio is very sweet, but you'll make a

mistake if you think he's reasonable. He knows women don't like to be interrupted. That soft look he gets in his eyes while you're talking? He's thinking about car races— or material things. He's counting up all his soft shirts and shiny shoes."

"I like his shiny shoes," Kitty said. "They make me feel well taken care of."

Alexandra suppressed a desire to excuse herself and go to her refrigerator. "How does Violet sound to you?" she said.

"Fine."

"That's what I think. Helena thinks she's getting into trouble. She wants me to warn her."

"I hope you told her it's bad manners to interfere in your friends' sex lives," Kitty said.

Alexandra took the pillow next to her, put it on her stomach and hugged it. "I don't know what's bothering her," she said.

"She has too much ambition and she's not using it. That's what's bothering her. She's leading an aimless life."

Alexandra said, "I wish my life were that aimless. At least she has a husband to pay attention to."

"She spends a lot of time on him, but I don't think that's real attention. Men don't have long affairs with their secretaries if their wives are really paying attention."

Talking about the ins and outs of marital relationships always brought up her own parents' very emotional marriage—which ended in a car crash when she was twelve—and made Alexandra want to change the subject. "If Helena doesn't suspect there's anything wrong, the affair doesn't make much difference anyway," she said.

"The poor man wants a family. He'll be lucky, once she has a baby, if she has any time for him at all."

Alexandra picked a big, fuzzy white feather out of the pillow on her stomach and ran it under her nose. It felt like someone's breath. "You know," she said, "Rebecca could be planning to get pregnant, too. Did you ever think of that? Or do you think the competition would be good for Helena?"

Kitty said, "I don't think John will ever leave Helena. He's too turned on by her helpless act. He feels very manly taking care of her even though she's ordering him around."

"I think he stays with her because she gives good head," Alexandra said.

"Haha," said Kitty.

Alexandra said, "Maybe Helena's bored with John. He's getting fat. You never see them talk to each other anymore."

"Talk isn't everything," Kitty said.

"I can't get close to a man if he doesn't have anything to tell me," said Alexandra. "That's why I couldn't stay with Giorgio. There was nothing I could learn from him. He's sweet, but he's a very young soul."

"I've had a night to remember," Violet said to Kitty. She sat naked on her pink sheets with her knees up, exposing herself to the cool breeze that came from the air conditioner at all hours. It was 4:30 A.M. Wednesday in Los Angeles, and she hadn't spoken to a woman friend for almost two days.

"It's morning here," said Kitty. "I'm having a nettle tea and lavender bubble bath. Mmm, it feels great."

Violet could hear Kitty's body heaving around in the water, as if to remind her of how unreal she herself felt, purged of all passion and filled with the foreign substances, cocaine, champagne and gism. "I just made love with Roger Rathbone for the past three hours," she said.

"Congratulations," said Kitty. "I just put newspaper down for Aphrodisia."

"Aphrodisia?"

"The Whippet. They're not the kind of dog you can cuddle up to, but they run thirty-five miles an hour. That's practically as fast as an Italian sports car."

"I don't believe it," Violet said. "You mean you bought a Whippet to make Giorgio happy."

"No. Giorgio bought a Whippet to make me happy."

"Lucky you." Violet picked a long red hair—one of her own—out of her mouth. She hadn't called Kitty to hear about dog walking, but to recall the ecstasy of her sexual encounter by talking about it. "I hope I didn't get pregnant," she said.

"You should keep a spare diaphragm in your suitcase."

"I had my diaphragm, but I couldn't use it. Last night I told Roger I couldn't go to bed with him because I was faithful to Philip. Tonight I told him I couldn't resist him. He never would have believed me if he found out I brought my diaphragm to Los Angeles."

"My Aunt Rosemary worked for a gynecologist," Kitty said. "She used to say women never got pregnant unless they wanted to."

"That can't be right or I wouldn't have had two abortions." The thought of the lovely children, Philip's and hers, who would never have a chance to grow up because she was too selfish, filled Violet's eyes with tears. "I do love Philip. I don't think I'm serious about Roger. He's too insane. On the other hand he's a very interesting lover." At times like this, when she wanted everything, Violet suspected she was lacking in moral fiber. Some people, like Helena, never seemed to misbehave. Then again, they never seemed to be tempted. Where was the morality in that? "I don't know how I got into this mess. It's all because I didn't want to eat dinner alone," she said.

"If that's what it was, I'm sure Philip will understand," said Kitty.

"When I eat alone I always feel as if people are staring at me. Why should a woman eat alone unless something terrible is wrong with her, or she's trying to pick someone up?"

"I think that's a romantic idea. Sometimes a woman wants to eat alone. If you take a book with you and show you're serious about reading it, no one will bother you."

"Oh, Kitty, no woman wants to eat alone," Violet said. "Eating alone is always second best."

"If you didn't have such romantic ideas about men it might be easier for you to deal with them," Kitty said.

"If I didn't have romantic ideas I wouldn't want to deal with men at all," Violet said. "Now, do you want to hear my story?"

"How long will it take?"

You had to be careful about Kitty's short temper in the morning, when she thought you were keeping her from getting to work. "You can stop me when you've had enough," Violet said. "On Monday night Roger took me out to dinner at the Pheasant's Nest. It's very new, very intimate, nobody there but movie people. Each booth is surrounded by plants so you feel like you're alone—but it turns out you're not alone, they can hear you at the next table. The food is American-grown game. The plants are set in dirt on the marble floor."

"I went to a dinner the other night where there were

plants set in dirt on the buffet table. The dirt looked too much like the chicken livers Veneziano," Kitty said.

Violet said, "I talked to Freddy in the morning and he told me to make the supreme sacrifice for Star-Time if I had to. I think he was kidding. That's the trouble with working for a so-called gay man. They like to think of women as great bitches. At the same time they're terrified you might do something to embarrass them; something female and messy the way you do every month when you have your disgusting period."

"But Freddy's not gay; he's married with three children. I had an affair with him."

"He might as well be," Violet said. "He doesn't trust me. Anyway, the whole day, while I was listening to Glenda Crane talk about Hollywood fifty years ago, one part of my mind was getting dizzy thinking about Roger. I thought, I'm away from home. Philip will never know. And then I thought, what if Roger and I fall in love? I could end up alone in a big house in Hollywood cooling my heels while he's working on location, and his job is to make love to beautiful movie stars."

"That's what I'd call the Baroque worry department," Kitty said.

"It never hurts to be prepared," said Violet. "Then I thought, what if it's just a fling? What if I want it more than he does. Will it change my relationship with Philip? Then I thought, I don't want him signing with Star-Time or not based on whether I'm a good lay. I thought, how will I know if I'm making love to him because I want to or because it's good business? Then I'd think about the way he looked at me in the hallway yesterday morning when I opened up for room service and I'd feel weak."

"It's the eyes, isn't it?" Kitty said. "They're almost too bright."

"Manic," said Violet. "Then I'd think, if he's really so wonderful, what's he doing picking up women on airplanes? I hate being confused about a man.

"Dinner was a disaster. People kept coming up to the table. I suppose I should have been impressed. I kept feeling he wasn't paying enough attention to me. That's why I started talking about Philip."

"Why'd you do that?"

"I don't know. To make me seem important, too." Violet shivered and pulled the covers over her. "Roger wasn't very interested in Philip. I thought about how I'd have to lie to Philip about Roger, and I started feeling really guilty. I thought, someone ought to invent a personal pocket psychiatrist. It would be as small as a pocket calculator and it would have complete information about your past in its memory. So you could punch out a description of the things you're feeling, and the personal pocket psychiatrist would give you a little printout explaining your mood and telling you what to do about it."

"That's a great idea."

"I know. I'm full of good ideas. Roger said goodnight to me in the hotel lobby again. I felt dismissed, the way I used to when I was seven, and I'd ask my mother too many questions and she'd tell me to ask my father even though my father wasn't home."

"Maybe hearing about Philip turned him off."

"A man who's really interested in a woman is willing to make a few passes before he gets anywhere. Rejection makes him try harder," Violet said. "I went right upstairs and called Philip. There was no answer."

"Are we getting to the seduction soon?" Kitty swished in her bathwater. "I have a lot to do today."

"Okay. This afternoon he grabbed my leg in the pool. It was like an electric shock. About two hundred people were lying around watching, or he could have had me right there," Violet said. "I didn't have my qualms about Philip anymore after our talk."

"Who? You and Philip?"

"Didn't I tell you I talked to Philip in the morning?" Violet felt hot, now. She pulled her covers off. "He was in his lab with his genes. He seemed so sweet and far away. I thought, while he's there and I'm here, someone might drop a bomb. I'd want to be in the arms of a man when it happened. I know Philip would agree with me if I could explain it to him.

"Anyway I'll spare you any more preliminaries. Roger and I had dinner at the hotel and went straight to my room. His eyes looked as if they had pinwheels in them."

"Too much cocaine," Kitty said.

"Just enough," said Violet. "He started very slowly taking off his own clothes."

"I like a man who wants to rip my clothes off," Kitty said.

"I used to feel that way when I was young. Now I think it's more dignified to get undressed yourself." Violet could feel her own heartbeat. She was coming to the part that both excited and dismayed her. "When you really want someone, are you ever afraid, just before the two of you undress, that something's going to go wrong—maybe his cock will be so small you can't feel it, or so big you can't take it?" she said.

"How could a cock be that big?"

"Well, when Roger got undressed, somehow he got his
cock between his legs so it looked like he didn't have one at
all. He stood there smiling at me. I was terrified. I thought,
if he's had some kind of bizarre sex-change operation, I'd
better give him a lot of space to tell me about it. So I got
into bed and propped myself up on the pillows and smiled
back. When he saw I wasn't going to scream, he let it pop
out. Do you think there's something wrong with him?"

"It sounds that way," Kitty said.

"He says the difference between him and someone crazy
is he knows exactly what he's doing. He does whatever
comes into his head so he won't flip out. He put on my robe
to see how it felt to be me. It's just as bad when he tries to
act normal." Violet arched her back and stretched her
shoulders. "He's so intense. As soon as he got into bed, before he even kissed me, he said, 'Tell me what you like.' He
knows he's supposed to do that.

"I said, 'Sweetheart, give me a chance to see what you
do, first.' "

Kitty said, "I think some men use that question hostilely.
They interrupt things to ask, just when you're beginning to
enjoy yourself. It makes you feel like you're not a modern
woman if you don't have a quick answer."

"Roger's actually very polite as a lover," Violet said.
"He refused to have an orgasm until I did. It took me a long
time, too, with him waiting for me."

"It's performance anxiety. They're passing it on to us. I
won't let any man tell me whether I should come or not. I
just do it, as fast as I can."

"The best thing about Roger is the way he talks in bed. I
don't care if it's acting. Torrid talk makes a woman feel
loved." Violet felt a surge of tenderness toward Kitty for
witnessing, through her eyes, Roger Rathbone's passion for

her. "I hope you're being feminine with Giorgio," she said by way of returning the favor. "He's Italian, you know. They like women who walk three paces behind them."

"All men do," said Kitty. "Or at least they think so. Actually, the women they're happiest with are the ones who rule them. Without seeming to, of course. Look at Helena leading John around in her ribbons and lace. He knows exactly what he should do next with her. That's important to men."

"You know what?" Violet had an idea. "Do you have any clothes with ruffles on them? I'll bet Giorgio would love you in ruffles."

Kitty said, "Not with a Whippet on a leash."

"You're right," said Violet. "It may be too late."

"Ruffles aren't Giorgio's thing. He likes clingy, sexy clothes."

"He doesn't like them on his mother, you can be sure."

"Giorgio doesn't need me to be his mother. He has a mother."

"Men are always looking for their mothers in other women," Violet said. "They want them to be just like their mothers, only entirely different. Roger gave me a pair of banana-flavored paper underpants before he left this morning. He asked me to wear them to dinner tonight. I'll bet his mother used to feed him bananas when his stomach was upset."

"Banana-flavored paper underpants—that must be a California dish," Kitty said. "And speaking of luxury foods, I'd better dry off and get to the store."

For a half hour before she fell asleep Violet imagined she was living in Hollywood with Roger. They had sex at least twice a day on a huge, round bed and she spent the rest of her time there putting on makeup, eating bonbons, listening to the radio and talking on the phone. Roger had a secret closet full of sex equipment. Philip was the gardener. Philip took off his muddy boots and his fogged-up glasses, and had sex with her when Roger was away making movies. She had no time to be anybody's press agent.

Helena thought daytime long-distance phone conversations were extravagant. When she called Violet the following afternoon it was because she couldn't get herself out of bed. "I need an old friend to talk to," she said, running her hand across her new pink-and-tan plaid silk bedspread. Silk had been the right choice; touching it always soothed her.

"Am I glad to hear your voice," Violet said. "I feel terrible. You're the closest thing I have to a real mother."

"Did somebody tell you?"

"Tell me what?"

"About my mother. She's in the hospital."

"I was talking about my mother. I didn't know your mother was in the hospital," Violet said.

"How could you? She just went in." Helena's eyes were so dry she felt as if there were sand in them. "She says she has chest pains. They say she's fine but they're doing tests. John thinks she just wants attention."

"Have you seen her?"

"This morning. She was in bedclothes with an oxygen tube in her nose. I felt awful, so I told her how pink-cheeked and healthy she looked. She said she wasn't healthy, she was flushed. I told her a joke I thought was very funny. The one about the carpenter who comes to the Pearly Gates while Saint Peter is on a lunch break and Jesus is taking care of admissions?"

"Tell me," Violet said. "I could use a good laugh."

"Jesus asks the carpenter what he's done with his life.

The carpenter says, 'Not much. I've worked as a carpenter. I had one son and I lost him.' Jesus can hardly believe it. He searches the man's face. He says, 'Father?' The carpenter says, 'Pinocchio?' "

Violet said, "Hahaha."

"My mother didn't laugh either," Helena said. "Maybe it's the way I tell it."

"Maybe the subject was scary for her."

"She never laughs at my stories. I wish she were a sweet old lady I could do things for." Actually Helena wished her mother were at her bedside, laying a cool hand on her forehead. "I took her some Chanel Number Five cologne," she said. "She told me it irritated her nasal passages. She's been wearing it for twenty-five years. She said she'd give it to Flora, her nurse, if I didn't mind. I did mind, but I didn't say so. I'm scared. It's not like her to be lying down. What if she dies?"

"She won't be able to bully you anymore," Violet said.

"I'm used to it. Anyway, she's not a bully, she just wants me to be perfect." Helena sat up straight. "Of course, you could say it's not fair to have ambitions like that for your children. The truth is, sometimes I think she hates me." As these last sentences came out of her mouth, Helena felt what she could only describe as a thrill. She hadn't known she thought such a thing until she said it. Now that she had said it, her forehead unknotted and her shoulders and arms came out of their hunch, as if they'd been flooded with a sweet liquid, the body's natural morphine John was talking about last week. "Probably I hate her sometimes, too," she said. "That must be why, when she's telling me what to do, I feel like a ten-ton truck is on my chest, preventing me from answering back. Still, I would never deny her."

"What do you mean?"

"Don't tell her I told you. Kitty hates her parents so much she's making up a new set to tell *Gossip* magazine about."

"Maybe they're not her type," Violet said. "I used to think my mother hated me. It wasn't anything that dramatic. I'm not her type. She's outdoorsy. I can't stay outdoors more than ten minutes at a time. My skin is too fair."

"Your skin isn't really fair," blue-eyed Helena said. "Only blue-eyed people can be fair-skinned. So I'm fair even though my hair is dark. It's a medical designation."

"My skin is as fair as skin can be."

"Not with those big brown eyes, dear."

Violet said, "My eyes were violet until I was six months old. That's how I got my name."

"We know it wasn't because you were shy."

"You sound like my mother, telling me who I am and who I'm not."

"You and my husband are the only people who ever speak of me as motherly," Helena said, "and you both had terrible mothers whose husbands died young. It's no wonder I'm afraid to have a child."

Violet said, "Roger Rathbone and I have been lovers. I'm flying home in a few hours. I hate leaving him here. I'm afraid to even pack the souvenirs of our romance. An empty, folded Between the Acts cigar packet and a half-eaten pair of banana underpants. What if Philip found them?"

"I'm not going to ask what banana underpants are," Helena said.

Violet said, "You must think I'm awful."

Helena took a long drink of water from the tumbler at

her bedside table. She did think Violet was awful. "Are you going to see him again?" she said.

"He's coming back to New York sometime in the next few weeks," Violet said. "I've told him he can't call me, but I gave him my number so maybe he will. He's a terrific lover. At least I think so. We did enough coke so I would have thought so even if he wasn't there."

"I've been married so long I don't know what a terrific lover means." Helena let a small, very feminine sigh escape her.

"I mean he's completely uninhibited and he's very thorough. He has great powers of concentration."

"You mean like a really rich flourless chocolate cake?"

"Not at all. Chocolate cake makes me sick."

"It all depends on what you like. John's an efficient man," Helena said.

"Roger's efficient, too. First kissing, then oral sex, then fucking. He brought a vibrator last night."

It would be easier to talk about sex with your friends if they didn't make it sound so vulgar. "That's not very romantic, is it?" Helena said.

"That's what I thought at first. I thought, he's come to play doctor with his own doctor's bag; I wonder who else he's used his instruments on. But it turned out to be a present for me. It's made of superrealistic flesh-colored plastic. It has three speeds and five attachments. I had to explain I already had one at home."

Helena felt as if there weren't enough air in her room. She took a deep breath. "Do you really use a vibrator? I thought they were for prostitutes and old maids," she said.

"You ought to get one," Violet said. "I use it sometimes

while I'm talking on the phone. Just time it so you can get off before you come."

This conversation was making Helena horribly uncomfortable. As far as she knew she had never had an orgasm in her life, and if she had she wouldn't have called it "coming," a term she found too easily familiar for a phenomenon so difficult to grasp. "Do you think you're more likely to conceive a child on the occasions when you've had an orgasm?" she said.

"I hope not. Where did you hear that?"

"It just makes sense to me. I mean, you're more relaxed."

"I'm not relaxed at all," Violet said. "I feel just like a cat in heat."

Helena got out of bed and opened a window. "I think you're depraved," she said. "How do you know what you're really feeling, anyway, if you're all coked up?"

"You still feel what you're really feeling. You just feel a little numb at the same time."

"Do you and Philip use it?"

"Philip likes marijuana. Why do you ask?"

"I was thinking about Philip."

"Don't worry about Philip," Violet said. "I talk to him every day. He'll never know the difference."

"That's the big issue, isn't it? I mean in the etiquette of adultery. If the injured party never knows the difference, has he been injured?" Helena got back into bed.

"I don't know what you're talking about." There was a snap in Violet's voice.

Helena said, "If I write an etiquette book I'm going to have a chapter on the etiquette of adultery."

"I thought if you wrote a book it would be about design."

"This *would* be. Elijah Gordon thinks it's a good idea."

"Elijah always comes on with me," Violet said.

"John's authors never flirt with me," Helena said. "Elijah and I always talk about intellectual things. I told him I think there wouldn't be any more wars if the world were designed right. It's only common sense. If people were sure which doors were entrances and which were exits, they'd use the right doors, wouldn't they? If things were set up so that standing in line was the only way to get where they were going, they'd stand in line. They wouldn't even fight if the lines were designed to be cheat-proof. You can expand that idea to include everything that happens in the world."

"I just won't go anyplace where I have to stand in line," Violet said.

Helena said, "Elijah said I ought to start with something small."

"He's so intelligent, I bet you could learn a lot having an affair with him. I wouldn't want to marry him, though. His wife has awful frown lines on her forehead."

"Poor Rusty," said Helena, who didn't even wish to discuss the possibility of Violet having an affair with Elijah. "Those are the hardest lines to get rid of. I wonder if she's tried collagen injections." She wrote the word *collagen* on the blank pad on her bedside table. Sometimes, when she was tired, she could see the shadow of a deep line forming between her own eyes. "Anyway," she said, "I told Elijah, because of my mother being sick I've been thinking about the design in etiquette. I think manners are as important to behavior as grammar is to civilized conversation. He said I should write about that."

"Well, I think it's a great idea for you to write about the etiquette of adultery, but I'm not married so what I'm doing isn't adultery."

"You're just getting upset about a technicality." If you'd

asked Helena, she would have had to admit she felt relieved now that her mother was off her mind and Violet was the one who was squirming. "I want to know what's the polite thing to do when you have one person who thinks you're his exclusively, and you're having an affair with somebody else," she said.

"What if you think he's having affairs with people all the time?" Violet said. "It's funny—now that I'm away from Philip, I haven't been jealous at all."

"That's because you have a new man."

"That has nothing to do with it. Didn't your mother teach you about adultery?"

"She never mentioned it. Not even when my father left her for another woman."

"Okay," Violet said. "The smart thing to do if you're married is not to let your husband find out, unless you want to break up your marriage. It's also the polite thing to do. Another thing, you shouldn't let his friends find out. Why should he be embarrassed when you're the one who can't control your appetites? Don't let your lover call you at home or send you flowers.

"Oh, God, this is bringing back my last year with Stan. Don't feel so guilty you can't enjoy yourself. Don't start being absent and giving your husband excuses. If anything, you should spend more time with him when you're having an affair with somebody else."

"If you do all that, when do you ever see the person you're having the affair with?"

"You asked me about etiquette," Violet said. "The fact is, having an affair isn't a particularly polite situation."

"How about the other man? What are your obligations to him?"

"Tell him how things really are with you. If you know. And try not to fall in love with him."

"Why not?"

"Falling in love complicates everything, that's all."

"But don't you go into it for the complications?"

"I went to bed with Roger because I couldn't resist," Violet said. "And because I feel empty when I'm by myself. I could never fall in love with him, though. He's an ego-maniac."

"He must be one of the most attractive men in the world," Helena said.

"You wouldn't like him," Violet said. "Out of bed he has very bad manners."

FIVE

Helena was beginning to get into passion. This new interest was brought on by the dreams she was having about
Roger Rathbone. She woke from the dreams feeling exhil-
arated. During the day, while she was sharpening pencils,
or getting a bottle of Perrier from the refrigerator, she
would think of Roger and get pangs in the abdominal area
near her uterus. Such pangs rarely occurred in connection
with John, though she tried to pretend he was a movie star,
too.

She continued to wear old-fashioned white cotton night-
gowns to bed to please John, and she continued to be grati-
fied by his agitation when he entered her, climaxed and
rolled over—never without patting her on the rump and
muttering, "Thank you, darling." But now she wondered if
she wasn't capable of her own passion after all.

One Sunday afternoon she walked for an hour: up Lexington Avenue to Eighty-eighth Street, down Park to Fifty-eighth, back to Sixty-ninth and Third to the big, solid prewar building where she and John had bought their duplex apartment seven years ago——the apartment she'd been filling so beautifully with the modern spirit in furniture. At the hour's end she'd decided this: if passion was what she wanted, she owed it to her marriage to try to find her passion in John.

Which was why, when she phoned Violet from her kitchen at six o'clock that Tuesday, Helena was pushing marijuana through a strainer. "I saw your friend Alice today," she said.

"What friend Alice?"

"She wears Mary Janes and has a hookah on her coffee table."

"Oh, you mean my dealer Alice. She's Harriet Adams's friend. I can't believe you called her."

"It was a little uncomfortable. After I'd introduced myself I realized I didn't know what you're supposed to say to a dealer. I said, 'I'd like to buy some marijuana.' There was a big silence on the other end of the line. You know how I hate to do the wrong thing. I thought, she's probably going to go to jail because of me. When they arrest drug dealers, do they arrest the people who happen to be buying drugs from them?"

"They almost never arrest anybody for grass anymore," Violet said patiently.

"You ought to explain that to Alice," said Helena. "When she finally spoke to me she said, 'The Mad Hatter is having a tea party here. You can come if you like at three o'clock.' Do you know whether her phone is tapped?"

"All dealers are paranoid," Violet said. "The one I had before Alice wanted you to say, 'Hey, what's happening, man?' when you called up. Then, if he had drugs in stock, he'd say, 'Hey, man, if you're in the neighborhood, drop in and we'll rap for a while.' Alice always invites you to a tea party."

"Well, I guess I'd rather go along with her game than be forced to talk hippie talk." Helena rubbed her dry *sinsimilla* buds back and forth against the sieve she usually used for sifting flour, and the clean marijuana fell silently into the white bowl beneath, making a soft, shit-colored mound.

Violet said, "How did you like her tea set?"

"I couldn't stay for tea. I was late for the masseur."

"The masseur?"

Helena hoped Violet wasn't going to embarrass her. "My back was bothering me," she said. "I went to Alexandra's masseur. The one who looks at the way you stand there and understands the source of your pain."

"Well, what's the source of your pain?"

"He didn't say. He just kneaded my backside."

"Did you take all your clothes off for him?"

"Yes, and it was perfectly all right since he kept his on. He was like a eunuch, anyway. I mean fat and hairless. He said the treatment would unblock my sexual energy." Helena grazed a finger on the sieve's sharp wire. "Ow," she said. She held her breath, wondering if Violet would want to delve into the question of blocked sexual energy.

"If I were lying naked on a table and a man was giving me incredible pleasure with his hands, I know my sexual energy would come unblocked," Violet said.

"Oh, Violet. A masseur is like a gynecologist. You don't think about sexual things around him."

"My gynecologist is very attractive," Violet said. "But let me ask you something, dear. John doesn't seem like a pot smoker to me."

"I'm the one who doesn't know how to do it. John used to hang around with jazz musicians in the fifties."

"I guess because he always knows more than anyone else, it's hard to think of him as young and hip," Violet said.

Helena said, "When you complain to a friend about the members of her family, you're holding her responsible for something she can't do anything about. You know very well John's not stuffy; he's terribly intelligent."

"He's never stuffy with me. If you weren't my best friend I'd think he was flirting," Violet said.

Helena didn't want to discuss John's faults before she'd even started making his dinner. "I don't know how to introduce this marijuana gracefully into our evening. I'm afraid John will be suspicious," she said.

"Suspicious of what?"

Helena sneezed. "That I think it might make sex more exciting. Do you think he'll believe me if I tell him I was walking along Park Avenue and a bag of marijuana fell at my feet from a high window?"

"Why not just say you want to do something different?" Violet said. "It might turn him on."

"I'm not the one who ever says those things. I think that's the man's responsibility, and so does John. When he wants sex he undresses me, takes me to bed and does it with me. I hardly have to think about it."

"It's fun to think about, isn't it?" Violet said. "Maybe you ought to take a lover. Philip seems so much dearer to me now that I have that maniac Roger to worry about."

At the mention of Roger's name Helena felt a stirring in

her abdomen. She didn't see any way to continue this conversation. "You know me," she said. "I believe in the simple life."

"Take my advice," Violet said, "and don't try to smoke
any grass until after you've got the dinner made."

Helena dumped her marijuana from its bowl back into
the plastic bag it came in and threw out the seeds and stems.
She thought of John's face with various expressions, looking for one that moved her. She couldn't wait to be too
stoned to think.

Alexandra was sitting on her bed, a half-eaten bowl of
hulled sunflower seeds between her thighs, when she
phoned Helena that night at 7:30. "I feel as if there's a sob
caught in my throat," she said. "I just got off the phone
with Henry Sweet. He calls me three times a day now, just
the way Giorgio used to. I don't know what's wrong with
me."

"You seem fine to me." Helena sounded like a no-
nonsense nurse. "Maybe you take your moods a little too
seriously."

Alexandra slowed her pace to demonstrate the gravity of
her situation. "There must be some reason," she said, "why
I can't get off the phone with men. I haven't been laid in six
months. Maybe it's because I hate my body."

"I'm making dinner for John," Helena said. "All his favorite foods. Baked Virginia ham, corn on the cob, sweet
potatoes, tomato salad, apple pie and ice cream. He loves
American things because he had to live in Germany until he
was eleven."

"I haven't had ham in three years," Alexandra said
mournfully. "What am I going to do? I don't lose weight, I
don't feel better. Henry wants me to go with him to his fast-

ing retreat. He calls it Nirvana. Do you believe it? I said, 'Henry, darling, that must be a joke. My Nirvana is going to be filled with food.' He says my system needs cleaning out. He can tell by looking into my eyes that I'm very toxic. I suppose the days are gone when men saw women's eyes as twin pools of light reflecting the soul."

"That reminds, me," Helena said. "I went to Olaf the masseur today."

Alexandra said, "Olaf is wonderful, but he doesn't work with diet. Henry says it all starts with diet—your exaltations, your depressions, all your emotions. If you don't eat the right things you won't get the right feelings, or anyway not at the right times."

Olaf said deep relaxation releases the sexual energies," Helena said. "But he seems totally asexual."

"Nobody's asexual in New York these days. Some people might abstain for their health, or for spiritual reasons." Alexandra grabbed a handful of sunflower seeds and poured them slowly into her mouth.

"Well, it helps me to think of him as asexual. Even so, I'm not telling John another man touched my body."

Alexandra was almost overwhelmed by the sweet, nutty taste in her mouth. She wanted to disappear with it into her own digestive system. "I have too much energy right now for the sex I'm getting," she said. "Henry says I'm really a spiritual being. I don't know why. I must have indulged my appetites too much when I was younger." She sighed deeply. "I was remembering a weekend I spent with Roger Rathbone once. We were so close it was like two sides of the same coin. We couldn't stop touching each other. At the end I felt as light as a puffball."

"If he's like that, how can Violet be juggling him with Philip so easily?"

"She's not as emotional as I am." Alexandra grabbed another mouthful of sunflower seeds to keep any emotions from coming up. It was no fun having more to give than other people could take. "I hope fasting doesn't release my sexual energies," she said.

"When are you going? Are you sure this isn't Henry's way of making a pass at you?"

"He says he's beyond sex. I think of that as a spiritual reason. Anyway, he has a staff at the retreat. The men and women live in separate buildings. There's hiking, and meditation, and Henry gives talks. I may go this weekend."

Helena said, "Mmm. Excuse me for interrupting but do you like walnut oil? I used it in my salad dressing. It tastes like walnuts."

Helena seemed warmer than usual, although less interested in what you were saying. If she were someone else, you would suspect she was having an affair. "I'll start my fast this weekend if the new cleaning woman doesn't come," Alexandra said.

"I thought you did housework as therapy."

"That was an excuse. I really hate the idea of someone else straightening up my mess. It's going to be like having a mother all over again. A Haitian mother. Anne-Marie."

"My housekeeper, Mrs. O'Reilly, would be perfect for you," Helena said.

Alexandra wondered if she'd eat fewer sunflower seeds if she took only two at a time. "If I had to call her by her last name I could never tell her what to do," she said. "Henry says I should stop thinking I have to be nice to everyone. He says being nice keeps me from being me."

"What if you really are nice?"

"I should be giving more love out," Alexandra said. "Being nice isn't the same thing as loving."

"Well, you don't have to love your cleaning woman. Just have a nice talk with her, right in the beginning, about how you want her to do things in your apartment. Remember, you're the boss."

Alexandra sighed. "I know my life is getting better, but I wish I didn't feel so awful. I'd like to be cheerful, like you."

"My mother brought me up to be cheerful," Helena said.

"Your poor mother. How is she?"

"They couldn't find anything wrong with her. We took her home from the hospital yesterday."

"That's great. Is that why you're celebrating tonight?"

"I'm not celebrating," Helena said. "Of course I'm relieved that she's okay."

"But all of John's favorite foods."

"That's for John and me. Because I'm glad he's my husband. And he won't believe me if I don't get off the phone and go pay some attention to him."

Alexandra didn't feel any better about herself when she hung up, but at least she had something new to think about. It sounded to her as if Helena were planning to have an affair with her own husband, without knowing there was someone else doing that already. She was dying to talk to a friend about it. First she'd visualize herself fasting and see if that lessened her desire for the macrobiotic takeout food she didn't plan to eat for another half hour. Then she'd call Kitty. No. The idea of calling Kitty made her desperately hungry. Do the visualization, then call Henry, and avoid, for the moment, the subject of Giorgio and his wonderful capacities.

Kitty phoned Helena from her bedroom at 8:45 that evening. "Men," she said. She sat on the polyurethaned parquet wrapped in a towel, pressing herself into the corner nearest the bed. "They just require too much attention. It's not bad enough that I have to listen to a daily recital of the sister's love problems and the mother's aches and pains. At least I can tell myself they don't live next door. It would still take them a day to get here from Milano. I mustn't forget how much I love being loved on a regular basis. But I never said I needed a dog to remind me of the man when he was gone. She doesn't leave me alone. If she's not trying to lick my face, she's wagging her tail at my porcelain animals, or shitting on my rug. When I rub her nose in it, she looks at me as if she's nobler than I am. I'm not interested in taking care of animals, or I would have stayed on the farm."

There was a forty-five-second silence on the other end of the line. Then Helena said in her most definite manner, "No one should give anyone else a pet for a present unless they're sure they want one."

"I'm afraid I told him I'd adore a dog," Kitty said. "In the heat of passion."

"My husband and I just finished dinner," Helena said. "I made a meal of his favorite foods. He left half his ham over. He's cutting down on fats, he said. When I try to tell him to cut down on fats, he thinks I'm treating him like a middle-aged man. He is a middle-aged man, but I can't say that. Now he's in the living room playing scales on his flute. I'm stacking the dishwasher. I'm worn out."

"Anyway, I got you at a good time," Kitty said.

Helena said, "I have a pipe and some marijuana for us to smoke. I've always heard it makes everything seem like more fun than it really is. If that's so, why would he tell me it puts him to sleep? I hope you don't mind, I said you gave it to me."

"If it's for sex, you ought to try cocaine," Kitty said.

"Not me." Helena's voice went up an octave. "I don't want to turn into a drug addict. I just want to relax."

"It's hard to relax when you're dealing with a man," Kitty said. "They have such tender egos. They want to feel like they're in control all the time. But I think letting a man control the situation is a sexist act."

"I like knowing John can take care of me," Helena said in her little-girl voice.

Kitty straightened up into the cross-legged lotus position. "Giorgio and I are having a real battle," she said. "At first he thought he could make arrangements for our evenings without consulting me. Now we have one conversation every day just devoted to the evening. So we've worked that out beautifully, but he still wants to pay my way. He thinks if he pays then he can be the one who makes decisions. I know what I'm talking about. That's the same reason I want to pay."

"It's nice, sometimes, to have someone else tell you what to do," Helena said pensively. "It gives you a sense of direction."

"Giorgio wants it to be his responsibility when things go right and mine when things go wrong."

"There are times when I feel like I don't know who John is at all." Helena lowered her voice. "This is confidential," she said. "Though I don't know how long I can keep it a secret. He's turning into a fire buff."

"A fire buff. John? You mean he's been setting fires?"

"Of course not. That's a firebug. A fire buff is someone who loves fires and fire fighters. It's just my luck we have a firehouse on the next block. John's started to visit there on his way home from the office. He says he wants the fire fighters to be his friends because they're genuine heroes, and they take their heroism for granted. He's trying to get them to let him go along on the fire truck as if he were one of the boys. I don't want anyone to see him riding on a fire truck, pretending to be one of the boys."

"Don't worry," Kitty said. "They don't have room for civilians on the fire truck."

"He could get killed." Helena lowered her voice again. "I said to him, 'A man who writes a book that's good enough to be published is a genuine hero. Why can't you think of your authors as heroes and leave the firemen alone?' He said fire fighters were men of action; his authors were always sitting around complaining.

"Just now he told me he's going to have dinner at the firehouse tomorrow night. Gino is cooking, the gourmet Italian chef fire fighter. We have a party at the Armstrongs tomorrow night. He asked me to make his excuses. There might be a book in the great chef fire fighters. I think it's the uniforms that excite him. They remind him of World War Two."

Kitty pictured John Welles in a fireman's hat, tramping up a tenement staircase axe in hand, yelling orders to the tenants in his German accent. "Maybe it's just a passing fad," she said.

Helena said, "He's such a tenderhearted man."

"You probably want to get back to him, too," Kitty said. "And I'm expecting a call from Judy Thaxter. I want to ask your advice."

"Who's Judy Thaxter?"

"The *Gossip* reporter. You talked to her at my party."

"Oh, yes, the one who had ball-point pen on her blouse."

Kitty's back felt tired. She got on her bed and lay down flat to rest it, but lying down on the bed made her want Giorgio when she was having a night off. She sat up again.

"I don't know whether or not to put Giorgio into my story," she said.

"Wouldn't it be simpler not to? What if you're not with him when the story comes out?"

Helena was so literal. Why didn't she know that women said negative things about their lovers to get positive feedback from their friends? "I'd like some pictures of us together," Kitty said.

"I wouldn't want anyone to know who I was sleeping with if I wasn't at least engaged to him," Helena said, "but I suppose I'm old-fashioned."

"That's why marriage is so good for you," said Kitty sweetly.

"I guess so. I wish I knew how John knows marijuana makes him sleepy. He hasn't had a puff he's told me about in the eight years we've known each other."

Kitty said, "You're awfully wound up tonight."

"I was looking forward to a romantic evening at home, but the telephone keeps interrupting."

"You could put your machine on."

"I know. But I don't want to miss anything."

"Do yourself a favor," Kitty said, "and don't smoke that grass until you get yourself into a good mood."

"I'll be in a great mood," Helena said, "as soon as I finish cleaning the kitchen. I hate to look at a mess."

"Call later if you want to talk," Kitty said, and she hung up before Helena could tell her how looking at a mess made her feel.

When Violet phoned Helena at 9:30, she told herself she'd get right off the phone if Helena didn't want to talk. "I hope I'm not interrupting anything," she said. If she had to she could always watch television until she fell asleep.

She was in bed already, with the TV on and the remote-control wand in her hand.

"We just smoked some grass," Helena said.

"That's great." Violet punched the TV sound down. "It will take a little while before it gets to you."

"I feel funny already. It's almost as if everything that happens is part of a movie I'm watching."

Violet was glad she'd phoned, after all. Helena needed encouragement. "Go with it," she said.

"But it's the opposite of being too stoned to know what you're doing. Too stoned to know what you're screwing. That's funny." Helena giggled.

"I have a great story to tell you," Violet said.

"Everybody has to talk tonight. It must be the full moon."

Maybe Helena was right not to smoke grass if it made her sarcastic. "At least let me go first," Violet said. "I'm the one who called."

"I was just massaging John's feet when the phone rang," Helena said. "Through his socks. They felt so warm."

"This will only take a minute. I saw Roger this afternoon," Violet said.

"Oh, yes?" You could hear Helena relaxing into the conversation. "How come you didn't tell me before?"

"Because I can't stand him. He's so inconsiderate. He asked me to meet him after lunch at the bar of the New Cairo Hotel. I told Freddy we were talking public relations. It could have been a perfect rendezvous, but naturally Roger was late. A man should never let a woman wait unprotected at a bar. She's likely to pick someone up just to make herself feel respectable. There was a very attractive man sitting three seats away from me, and believe me I was tempted. Luckily the bartender wanted to talk. When Roger finally got there he interrupted the bartender's story about his sister who sells cosmetics door to door—and makes a fortune, by the way. I might want to go into that business if public relations doesn't pan out." Violet saw herself in her long hair and high-heeled sandals carrying a sample case through a treeless suburban street, and she squared her shoulders.

"You wouldn't have met Roger if it hadn't been for public relations," Helena said.

"That's what I mean. He's a movie star, but he acts like an orangutan. I could find a nice truck driver who'd treat me with more respect. He wouldn't even let me finish my drink. Why should I quench my thirst and settle my nerves when he wants to drag me off to his room? I guess I still want him because he wants me so badly. But that's the only time he thinks about me—when his cock reminds him. The rest of the time, Roger is the only person on his mind. You know what a fast talker I am. I'm like a geisha around him. The worst of it is, while I'm feeling bad that I can't get a word in edgewise, I'm also feeling bad because that's the way Philip must feel around me. I'd die if Philip left me."

"John's got his shoes back on," Helena said. "I've got to get off. I hear him walking down the hall."

Violet fully supported Helena in her wish to stay married to stuffy, two-timing John Welles, if that was what she wanted. Still, she didn't believe in wasting opportunities. "He's going to the bathroom," she said. "Just talk to me until he gets out."

"I want to make sure I get off the phone in time," Helena said. "There was something I wanted to say, though." She paused. "I know," she said. "About people leaving people. Sometimes things change between people without them even knowing it."

"Stop it," Violet said.

"Or being able to stop it," Helena said. "I was looking at John a few minutes ago, and he looked like an owl to me."

"I can see that. The dark-rimmed glasses and the big, serious eyes."

"Why hasn't he looked that way before? He was looking back at me. His eyes were sad. I thought, he'll never hunt again. He's lost the killer instinct. Oh, Violet, I want to cry."

"It's the grass," Violet said. "Just feel what you feel and the feeling will go away."

Helena said, "John is back in the living room. He's put the radio on."

"I'll let you go in one minute. Just let me tell you what I decided tonight. I have to know what you think." Violet watched two cars chasing each other across the TV screen. "I think I figured out why Philip and I fight," she said.

"You mean because you never consider his feelings?"

"Not at all."

"I thought that was what you said a few minutes ago."

"You know grass makes you a little abrasive," Violet said. "You have no idea what it's like when Philip and I are together. I think the whole problem is I defer to him too much."

"You defer to him too much?"

"I mean I've always thought you're supposed to do things the man's way if you want to keep him happy. So I try to figure out what he wants and then I pretend I want it, too. Then I get mad because I'm not getting things my way. That's why we fight. I used to do the same thing with Stan. Only we were married, so I was ironing shirts for him, too, and not getting any thanks because his laundress used to do a better job."

"I love ironing John's shirts," Helena said.

"I knew you were going to say that."

"I don't have the time now that I'm thinking about writing a book. But sometimes when I'm thinking about writing I wish I were ironing shirts. It's so satisfying to take something wrinkled and make it smooth."

Violet said, "Even when I try to do what Philip wants, I don't really know what he wants. It dawned on me tonight that I could save a lot of energy if I just told him what I wanted. Do you think that would be too unfeminine? Roger's been giving me such a hard time I'd like someone to be good to me. He could tell me what he wanted, too."

"Say you wanted different things. Would you do what you wanted, or what he wanted?"

Violet could see she wasn't going to get any sympathy out of Helena tonight. "I'll worry about that later," she said.

"I think you have a great idea," Helena said. "Now you'll have to excuse me. I want to join my husband in the living room."

Violet had intended to be the one to end the conversation. "I've got to go, darling," she said. "I must call Philip before it's too late."

Helena felt better once she'd got Violet off the phone, and could concentrate on herself. Her whole body seemed to be pulsing slightly. Pulsation must be a natural rhythm. She smiled to think she had such a thing in her thin, tense body. John would be waiting in the living room for her to touch him with her rhythm. She moved in a sort of samba step down the hall.

Though John was in the living room, he wasn't waiting anymore, he was sleeping. This was nothing unusual. The sight of John asleep in his chair, with his head thrown back and his neck exposed, was a visible symbol their marriage was a success from his point of view. What was unusual was the extent of her disappointment. Also unusual was the picture that flashed through her mind and was gone—her delicate hands around his throat applying pressure, his eyes bulging, his tongue hanging out. His tongue was blue.

Almost at once she recognized her fury as a passion, and in her intoxicated state she imagined she could use it to create the passion she desired. She'd wake John and discuss it with him. They'd smoke some more, and maybe she'd open up and conceive. First she rubbed herself gently in the area of her genitals, an ordinarily useless activity John always performed out of courtesy. The warmth that radiated through her body came as a shock. She felt like a very bad girl.

John's big head shifted its weight on the chair back as if he'd heard Helena's thoughts. He snored three times, then stopped with his mouth open. His snores were a comfort to her. She'd better put on the phone machine. She acted, so it seemed, not a moment too soon. The telephone rang.

"Mrs. Welles," the woman's voice said into the machine, "this is Flora James at Saint Anne's Hospital. Your mother's come back. They think it's a heart attack. She may not last the night."

Helena picked up the receiver. "Tell her I'm on my way," she said in a commanding voice, but the nurse had already hung up.

SIX

Alexandra called Violet about a week later. "I'm going to do a monologue on my radio show tomorrow," she said. "Could you do me a big favor and tell me what you think of it?"

"I'd love to, but Freddy doesn't allow radios in the office," Violet said.

Alexandra's throat felt scratchy right behind her tonsils. "I mean now," she said.

"Now?" Violet said. "I guess so. Can you hold on while I get a blanket? I'll freeze if I sit still in here tonight." Alexandra took a drink of water, filled the glass again, and sat down at her kitchen table. Violet picked up the phone. "Philip's having dinner with some scientists," she said. "I can't get comfortable. Ames Elliot called just before you did. The banker I've known since last fall. He invited me to a black tie dinner for Ames James. They're cousins on their mothers' sides. It sounds great, but I can't lie to Philip. So I probably don't have room in my life for Ames."

"It's no fun to be sensible, is it darling?"

Violet sighed emphatically. "Please do your monologue," she said.

"Thanks. Wish me good luck," said Alexandra, and she tuned out the sounds of Violet's petulance and imagined herself behind her pink circular desk in her studio, with her personalized silver earphones on, speaking low into her shiny silver microphone. She let her mind take off as if it were flying, and projected her voice as if it were the wind, whispering into every listener's ear.

"Hi, darlings," she said. "Today I'm going to talk to you about food. I don't know how many of you know it, but food is one of my favorite subjects. Food and eating. We all need to eat to live. Some of us live to eat. Nothing tastes as good as food. Food makes you warm, it fills you up, it stops that empty feeling in the pit of your stomach.

"I know because I've been empty for three days. Three whole days, can you believe it? Last weekend I went on a fasting retreat.

"Now, you're probably saying to yourself, 'Why would anyone want to fast if food is one of her favorite subjects?' Two reasons, darlings. I thought it was time to give my digestive system a rest. And I wanted to break the eating habit, and recapture my rapture over food. Some of you may know what I mean. Any time you have any disappointment, or you want to reward yourself, or you're just tired, you go to the refrigerator and stuff something into your mouth. You don't even taste it after the first few bites. Eating is just a habit.

"I want to talk to you about the joy of eating.

"Eat, drink and be merry, darlings, but the food you eat goes right into your bloodstream, so it's important to eat the right things. And I don't mean just health foods. Before I went on my fast I was eating only health foods. I felt a heaviness in my heart. I thought it was depression, but it stopped when I stopped eating all that heavy bread. And all those lumpy things made out of beans.

"Don't misunderstand me. The bean is a magical food, especially the soybean. The soybean is capable of transformation. They make it into a meat substitute, a cheese substitute, a butter substitute, a milk substitute. But you notice no one ever eats the soybean for itself.

"Why not? Because it's heavy and gritty, and there's no gaiety about it. Any of you who've ever been to a health food restaurant will know what I mean. Why do you have to speak in hushed tones in a health food restaurant? Why do all the customers look down at the mouth? I think it's because they're eating too many beans. I think it's because they're treating the food with too much reverence. Food isn't medicine.

"While I was fasting, darlings, believe me, I never once craved a veggie burger, or a slab of tofu-carob pie. I thought about Chinese food and Italian food and French food, and steaks and lobsters and ducks and curries and chilies. I smelled the smells, and when they started to overpower me, I thought about the rituals of eating food.

"Do you pick up your rice bowl in a Chinese restaurant because that's what the Chinese do? I'm not sure if that's right unless you're Chinese, too. I'll take calls about that, but not today, darlings. Today I'm talking to you about chop chop. Don't you love chopsticks? Even if I didn't like Chinese food I'd go to Chinese restaurants so I could use chopsticks. Speaking of chopsticks, don't ask for them in a Thai restaurant. At home the Siamese people eat with spoons and forks.

"And what about eating spaghetti? I go to Italian restaurants so I can twirl spaghetti around my fork. No big spoon there, please. And, dig it, if you ever have a chance, go and eat out Ethiopian. They give you hot food and a pancake, and they tell you to eat with your hands.

"I'm getting very hungry, how about you? Do you know how to eat a sandwich in a pita bread? It looks like a sweet little envelope, but whenever I pick one up and bite into it, I get dressing all over my face and stuffing all over my hands. I saw a diagram in a magazine once, showing you which bite to take first, and which next, and which after that. I didn't have time to memorize it, so I just cut my pita sandwiches on my plate as if they were crepes, or omelets. Call if you have a better answer, but not now, darlings. On Thursday.

"Actually I don't mind getting dressing all over my face and stuffing all over my hands. I'm just embarrassed to do it in front of other people. Tell the truth. When you're at home alone, don't you ever slurp your soup straight from the bowl, or stick a finger in the peanut butter jar, or maybe you like to lick the gravy from your plate.

"Did you ever dream of wallowing in a tub of chocolate-chocolate-chip ice cream? I had that dream while I was fasting, darlings. The chocolate was seeping into all my pores. I thought I had died and gone to heaven. Then they woke me up for the morning's meditation.

"Now, maybe for you meditating is like wallowing in a tub of chocolate-chocolate-chip ice cream. As for me, I've finally come to realize meditation is not my path. I have a hard time getting high on the sounds in my head. I don't even like sitting still.

"When you're fasting at this fasting retreat—they call it Nirvana to remind you of all there is to aspire to—they try to initiate you into the simple life. You sleep on a cot, and drink spring water, and take long walks in the woods. I went there prepared to turn into a nun.

"My dear friend Henry Sweet gives seminars every night there on the healing powers of love. Every night, the traditional time for making love on a personal level, you're tuning in to universal love. Henry says if you can really love every creature in the universe, starting with yourself, your family and your friends, you'll never eat too much again.

"Now Henry's a man who practices what he preaches. I used to think he loved me in a special way. There were ten women fasting at Nirvana with me, and he loved each of us equally. He gave us equal time. We were all special to him. You know me. I tried to hog him for myself, as if he were my own private philosopher—or a tub of chocolate-chocolate-chip ice cream. I had so many things to discuss with him. I tried everything. But everything he had to give me he had to share with all the women, just the way I'm sharing my experience with you, now.

"You're probably saying to yourselves, What's got into Alexandra? She's talking a blue streak today. Listen, it's not what's got into her, it's what's cleaned out.

"Let me tell you something, darlings, you owe it to yourself to try fasting. Lighten up your life. Clean yourself out, get rid of the toxins in your body. Flush them out with spring water. No matter how good the food tastes going down, there are waste products that get stuck inside of you. Can you imagine? Parts of that lobster you had with your boyfriend in Maine five years ago might still be there, festering in a pocket of your small intestine, sending out toxins and getting you down.

"Dig it. I'm not depressed anymore. No more tension headaches. I feel so hungry I could eat a horse. Don't worry, darlings, that's just an expression. I hardly eat any red meat at all.

"You learn the difference, when you're fasting, between eating to satisfy your appetite and eating to stuff yourself. You enjoy the taste of food again. Doesn't the thought of food make the tip of your tongue tingle? Apples, bananas, peaches and cream, lemon meringue pie, Boston cream pie, cream of tomato soup—did you have that at school when you were a kid?—leek and potato soup, vichyssoise, eggs à la Russe, cheddar cheese omelet, tuna cheese casserole, macaroni and cheese, spaghetti and meatballs, lasagna, linguine with clam sauce, linguine with pesto, linguine with garlic and oil—darlings, I'll eat Italian food any way they serve it. It's healthful and it's also joyful. Italian food must be my favorite. In moderation, of course.

"Here's the point. I know you like it when I make a point, don't you? Whatever is nourishment for you, whether it's food, or reading, or looking at paintings in museums, or playing baseball, or making love, take a rest and find out what it means to you. See how well you can do without it. Fill your time with other things. Don't let yourself be desire's slave. Desire's slave, darlings. It sounds thrilling, doesn't it? But we all know bondage hurts. Eliminate desire from your life, and you can have everything you want. Think about it." Alexandra stopped. She felt as if she'd stripped all her clothes off, spiritually speaking, down to her filmy underwear.

"Is that it?" Violet said.

"That's it."

"Did you make it up as you went along?"

"Yes and no, darling. I knew what was on my mind. What

came out wasn't any accident." Alexandra sighed. "Did you like it?"

"I'm not that mad for food," Violet said, "but I can't imagine life without desire. I want Roger all the time when I don't want Philip, and sometimes I want both of them at once."

"And Ames is waiting in the wings."

"Ames isn't waiting in the wings. I'm not attracted to Ames. I'd just like to get to know him better because he's so rich."

"You know you'd feel stronger if you weren't so dependent on sex," Alexandra said.

"I wish I had my own guru," said Violet.

"Sometimes you're very mean," Alexandra said. "To be around someone who practices universal love is a high experience. He's completely open to you, even if nothing happens."

"Then you still have impure thoughts."

Alexandra got a sudden pain in her ascending colon. "Do you mind if we talk more later?" she said. "I'm absolutely drained."

Alexandra's monologue made Violet feel like eating junk food. Imagine one woman telling another to give up sex, just because she wasn't getting any. Women would never be totally trustworthy friends as long as they thought they knew what was best for you. She picked up the phone and called Kitty. "Here's a juicy tidbit," she said. "Alexandra made a pass at Henry at the fasting retreat this weekend. He turned her down."

"Poor Alexandra," Kitty said. "I guess he's kind of attractive if you like boring Middle Western good looks."

"He told her he was into universal love."

"I don't really have time to gossip right now," Kitty said. "Giorgio's here waiting to take me and the dog for a walk."

"If I were you I'd keep my eye on Giorgio, darling. Take him and the dog to the country. Alexandra's getting ready to strike again."

"Did she say that?"

"I just have an intuition," Violet said. "Trust me."

"It's all over between them. Not that there was anything between them to start with. Giorgio loves me. I'm the one who's not sure how I feel about him," Kitty said.

Violet said, "She told me Italian was her favorite food. I think she had Giorgio in mind. That's all. *Ciao.*"

Violet felt better when she hung up. The alarm she'd stimulated in Kitty functioned like emotional spring water, flushing the irritation out of her own system as if it were so much toxic waste.

SEVEN

Helena called Kitty first when she and John came back from Connecticut. It was Tuesday, noon. She was in her workroom, curled into one corner of the hardwood, splatter-painted Italian chair that looked like a carved Victorian armchair flattened by a steamroller. The chair was more fun to look at and think about, really, than to sit in for very long. She skipped the formalities. "My mother's on my mind all the time. Last night John was driving and I was talking about her, and he started to fall asleep at the wheel," she said. "I'm not kidding. She's being discharged from the hospital in a few days. Then she'll go to a rehabilitation center. It's called Heart Throb House. They'll teach her about diet and exercise and resuming a normal life, but I'm afraid she's too old to live alone. That's how she had the heart attack in the first place."

"People have heart attacks from eating too much choles-
terol, not from living alone," Kitty said.

"Didn't I tell you how it happened? Right before she
started having her chest pains she heard a crash in my old
bedroom. She was sure a rapist had gotten in. The first pain
came while she was looking for the gun. At her age she
shouldn't have to think about shooting anybody. She man-
aged to get herself and the gun to my room. Poor thing, she
says she was trembling. She pushed open the door and the
room was empty. What she'd heard was my high school
graduation picture crashing to the floor.

"John says it can't be my fault since I wasn't there. But
that's the whole point. I wasn't there. She bent down to put
the picture back on the desk and the pain was terrible."

"This is a terrible story," Kitty said.

"I know. That's why I can't stop thinking about it. She
was on her way to get a broom to sweep up the broken glass
when she broke out in a sweat. Her friend Frances Nichols
broke out in a sweat when she had a heart attack. My
mother called the ambulance. We've reframed the picture
and put it back on the desk while she's been gone.

"I wish she'd invite her sister Louise to live with her. She
says Louise hates her. The only person she's ever been able
to live with in that apartment is me. At the hospital, every
time I told her I had to leave, or I couldn't come, she'd say,
'That's perfectly all right, dear, Flora is right here.' Flora's
the nurse she's teaching to be a lady. She'd say, 'It's Flora's
job to take care of me.' I felt so guilty I had to get away for a
few days."

"You don't think she was trying to get you off the hook?"

"Not my mother," Helena said.

Kitty said, "Excuse me a minute." She didn't go anywhere, though, she simply lowered her voice to a whisper;

Helena made out the words "dollars," "baby," "secretary," "loser." Then Kitty spoke into the phone again. "Listen, don't talk about this if you don't want to," she said gently, "but Violet told me your mother actually died and came back."

"Violet told you that?" Helena hated Violet. "That woman will do anything for a good line," she said. "Breaking the news when a friend's mother dies and comes back is as bad as breaking the news of a friend's engagement."

"So it's true?"

"My mother died and came back. They say so. They say her heart stopped for five minutes. My mother says she left her body. It's a little hard for me to imagine. She says she was a spirit flying around the room. From where she was her human self and all the doctors working on it looked pitiful. She was as light as the air because all her troubles were behind her. According to her, being human and being troubled amount to the same thing. Up there she was floating, just an essence—apparently still in human shape, since she was wearing an emerald tiara. She thinks they were preparing her to be a queen in the spirit world. A beautiful green light beckoned to her from above, and the sweetest voices sang. The way I used to sing before I got interested in riding horses, and lost my voice. A soft breeze came to waft her away. But even with all that joy there was something in her that couldn't go. She says she wanted to see me happy again before she died."

"I hope that doesn't mean if you're happy it will kill her."

Helena had thought all she could, for the moment, about her mother's motives. Her own were really much more interesting. She said, "When they told me she had died, I didn't cry. I didn't relive our happiest moments together.

I started to plan her funeral. We were in the hospital waiting room on those orange plastic-covered chairs. I read somewhere that orange is the color of insanity, but that doesn't make sense, does it? I turned to John and I said, 'Okay, you phone Oliver Mayo and see if you can't get an obituary into *The New York Times*. Tell him about her Poor Orphans' Foundation. I'll put a notice in the *Times* to run for three days. Instead of flowers, people can send contributions to the Poor Orphans.' "

Kitty said, sotto voce, "Tell her if she wants more than two dozen hens she can get a five percent discount. Two dozen, okay, sweetheart?"

"What?" Helena said.

Kitty said, "Sorry."

Helena said, "So anyway, I said to John, 'We'll have white lilacs all over the altar. The smell of lilacs always made Mother smile. I'd like to have the services at St. Stephen's. She stopped going to church years ago, but she'd want to be presented formally to God, if it turns out there is a God. The Reverend Poole will know her, if he's still alive. She wants to be cremated. She's leaving her ashes to me, along with the Limoges urn on her mantelpiece for me to put them in.' Did you know you have to buy a coffin anyway? They burn the body inside of it. Before they give you the ashes they get the coffin nails out with a magnet. I said, 'We might as well have her burned right away, and the ashes can be at the funeral. They put them in a nice little box with a veil over it.' Thank God we're Episcopalians so I didn't have to worry about the casket question. Proper Episcopalians have closed caskets."

Helena was dying for a nice, cold Perrier. Her mouth always got dry when she thought about the casket, and her silenced, embalmed mother packed inside it. "I knew exactly what to do about every detail," she said. "I suppose I'd been thinking about it, unconsciously, since she first went into the hospital. She'd expect me to make sure her funeral was done right. John was looking at me the way he does when I've just bought a new piece of furniture and he doesn't know what I'll do next. I said, 'She'd want all her friends to have lunch at her apartment, so we'll have the service in the late morning. I'll ask the organist to play Bach. Bill Eply should give the eulogy.' He's that very refined Latin teacher she takes to the opera. He adores her.

"The whole time I was doing this, I was thinking how pleased my mother would be with my performance if she could see me. I was in the middle of planning the menu—I thought we'd have Scotch salmon, and that warm chicken and broccoli you do, pepper Brie and arugula salad. I wasn't sure what to do about dessert."

"Hold on a minute," Kitty said, and she put Helena on hold. Helena breathed in through her nose, filling up her abdomen to the count of four, breathed out through her mouth to the count of eight, breathed in to the count of four. Being put on hold in the middle of a sentence was like having your plate cleared before you'd finished eating. Helena breathed out through her mouth to the count of eight. According to Alexandra, this deep-breathing exercise was good for relaxation and increased fertility. Helena breathed in to the count of four. Kitty came back on the line. "Plum tarts are very popular for funerals," she said.

"That's funny," Helena said, "I was thinking about plum tarts for my mother. Then they told me she wasn't dead after all, just resting. That was when I started to cry. John couldn't stop me. You know I love my mother, but I have to say this. It would have been just like her to die and come back, simply for the attention."

"It must be nice to have a mother who cares so much about you," Kitty said.

Helena sighed. She was bored to death with her mother. "I've been thinking about that," she said. "It's true she cares about me being a certain kind of person. That's supposed to be for my sake, but I think she just doesn't want a daughter who might embarrass her. Well, I hardly embarrass her. I'm thinking of writing a book about what she taught me. She didn't die; she's fine. I don't know why I feel like getting angry. I get an upset stomach when I get angry.

"John says I have a right to have it out with her. But what would I say after all these years? 'I hate you'? That's not polite. John says it's okay to blame her for giving me too many rules to follow, but I have to remember I'm the one who's followed them. The truth is, being right is probably my greatest pleasure in life—that and thinking about design. If I had children I'd teach them to do the right thing, too. So there's no one to be angry at."

Kitty said, "Giorgio calls his mother every day in Italy. He's a very good boy. Except that he hasn't told her about me. He says what's the point of upsetting her."

"Even though I may be upset I'm really glad I don't have to get angry," Helena said.

Kitty said, "I can't really get angry at Giorgio."

Helena straightened her body and stretched her legs. She was annoyed with Kitty for interrupting, but it wasn't really interrupting if she couldn't think of anything else she wanted to say. She said, "Do you want to marry Giorgio?"

"I want him to ask me. Let's take one step at a time. He's calling me twice as often now that I've put him into the *Gossip* story. I don't know whether he likes being linked with me, or if he just likes the idea of having his picture in a big American magazine. I have to talk fast because there are three suppliers waiting to see me and a dozen phone calls I have to make." Kitty lowered her voice. "I'm upset about Judy Thaxter. She's talking to everyone in New York, checking out my financial picture and my sex life. Maybe I'm being paranoid, but she's so sloppy about the way she wears her clothes—who knows what stories she may be picking up and dropping in the wrong places without even thinking about it. I'm getting calls from people I haven't seen in years.

"Today she told me she heard I was a lesbian and a coke-head and a Mafia front. At least she hasn't found my parents. I said to her, 'You must hear those things about everybody you interview.'

"She said, 'What's the veracity quotient in your case?' "

"Veracity quotient?" Helena said. She got up from her chair, stood straight and bent over from the waist, touching her right palm to the floor. The backs of her legs were stiff from sitting.

Kitty said, "Judy has a hard job, too. I said, 'Everything you've heard about me is true. Ask my mother.' I've already told her my mother is in a rest home in Florida.

"She could get me if she wanted to. It's not as if I never do coke. My first roommate in New York became famous as the girl-friend of a certain senator's wife. One of my partners is Italian. Not to mention my boyfriend."

Helena collapsed back into the chair. "But your partner's not a Mafioso and your roommate wasn't your girl friend," she said. Her mouth was parched. The things Kitty talked about made her feel as if she had to protect herself.

"I've never asked him where else he does business," Kitty said. "I never made it with Alison but I've made it with other women. There's hardly anything sexual I haven't done. No sheep, of course."

"You knew they'd investigate you before they started."

"I assumed they had some kind of etiquette about what they print and what they don't. But why would she be asking if she didn't want to print it?"

Helena couldn't stand Kitty's coyness about the attention she was getting. "Can you call it off?" she said, to be mean.

Kitty stopped. "I guess it won't hurt business," she said, "even if all those things come out. What I hate is the idea of people talking about me behind my back. Which reminds me. Did you hear Alexandra's food monologue?"

"When was this?"

"A few days ago. She got on the radio and talked about food for a half hour straight. Giorgio taped it. He's very proud of her. I sell food, and to me it's cuckoo to go on about it for that long nonstop," Kitty said. "Violet thinks Alexandra's pulling herself together. Call her up. I'll be interested to hear your opinion of her condition."

Sometimes Helena felt as if life were taking place inside an enormous hospital. "I'm going to have a few people out to my mother's house in Easthampton, weekend after next," she said. "John and I, really, but we're having my friends because I've just been through such an ordeal. Can you come? And do you want to ask Giorgio?"

Kitty said, "We'd love to. If I may speak for Giorgio."

Alexandra got down to business as soon as she heard it was Helena. "Hi, darling, you missed my food monologue," she said. "Did anyone tell you about it?"

Helena chose her word carefully. "Kitty said it was extraordinary." She found one loose end of the skein of pale pink wool next to her on the blue velvet sofa and began winding the wool around her finger to make a ball. She was going to knit a sweater for herself so she wouldn't feel use-less when she talked on the phone.

"She did? Extraordinary, huh?" Alexandra said. "I guess it was extraordinary. I hadn't eaten anything in days. It seemed as if food were the key to the universe. Maybe it is. I'll have to send you a tape. After I'd finished talking I felt totally depleted. I wasn't sure whether my audience could take it all in. You know, having an audience is like having children. They trust you completely."

"Having children couldn't be like having a radio audi-ence," Helena said.

"Maybe it won't be, for you. Anyway, they've all been calling the station. Now the station wants me to do more monologues. I'm trying to figure out how to do one on sex that they'll put on the air. I think food and sex are the same thing, don't you?"

Helena thought wrong thinking was what made Alexan-dra so unhappy. What was the point of talking about food and sex if you were going to deny them to yourself? "I think about furniture whenever there's nothing else in my head," she said. "Furniture is beautiful, and it never upsets you. In fact you can use it to make yourself comfortable."

"Giorgio loved the food monologue," Alexandra said in a softer voice. "He called me up to tell me. To him, he said, it was *favoloso*. That's Italian for fabulous. He said a man would like to be the inspiration for an outpouring of love like that. Isn't that beautiful?"

"What outpouring of love?" Helena was watching the way the skein of wool shriveled as her ball got bigger.

"You'll hear it when you get the tape," Alexandra said. "I never thought Giorgio listened to me. I thought he called me to listen to himself talking. I happened to say on the radio that Italian was my favorite food. He wants to take me for an Italian meal one night next week. He said I always looked like an angel sitting across the table from him. He didn't mean babyish and chubby, did he?"

Helena hoped she wasn't going to have to worry about taking sides again. Why couldn't Giorgio make up his mind? "What will he tell Kitty?" she said.

"I told him I couldn't go because of Kitty. How was your weekend alone with John?"

"We took long walks. I read Edith Wharton. She makes tragedy seem so painful. John read manuscripts and played Scrabble with himself. We ate good meals. John gives me everything I want. I guess that's wedded bliss." Helena sighed.

Alexandra sighed, too. "Wedded bliss," she said.

"You single women have exciting lives," Helena said. "You think married life would be more of the same, but it isn't. You're stuck with one man—listening to his ideas, putting up with his problems, doing things his way, watching him eat too much and fall asleep in his chair. What if you get bored? If John and I were divorced, I don't know if I'd ever marry again." The mention of divorce caused Helena to speed up the tempo of her wool winding. "Of course, I love John, so marriage doesn't bore me," she said. She lost her grip on the ball; it fell to the floor and rolled under the glass coffee table. She retrieved it and started winding again.

Alexandra said, "I bet you got pregnant while you were away."

"I didn't," Helena said. "It was the right time of the month. I read that book you gave me, *Joyful Reproduction*. I tried to think of myself as the beach and John's sperm as the ocean so when the moment came I'd let it wash into me. But I kept thinking about being at the beach with my mother when I was a little girl. She never wanted me to go into the water. It was too cold, or it was full of jellyfish, or there were sharks. I couldn't let him near me.

"Darling," Alexandra said, "how is your mother? I was so busy talking I forgot to ask."

Helena couldn't help it. Whenever anyone asked about her mother she pictured her propped up in her hospital bed waiting for the phone to ring. "She's fine," she said. "She's going to a terrific rehabilitation center in two days. They told her I had laryngitis and had to go away and rest. John had to go, too, to talk for me. I was worn out from listening to her for thirty years."

"I thought you were thirty-four."

Single women were always obsessed with age. "Thirty-four years. I had to get away. Her favorite nurse, Flora James, took care of her. You should see how Flora's manners have improved since she met my mother."

"At least your mother brought you up right. My mother never wanted to be a mother. She wanted to be a child. She was jealous of me because I was a child. She'd take me shopping for clothes with her and ask me what she should buy. On the bus she'd ask me to read aloud to her. She didn't care who overheard. She thought children like her shouldn't be disciplined. If I ever got angry with her, she punished me. Then one day she drove my father over a cliff. I had to be a total adult as a child. That's why I'm so childish now," Alexandra said. "Henry says I have to become my own parent. I suppose he's right."

Helena said, "If you want to get married, why don't you marry Henry?"

"Henry's into universal love."

"Uh huh. Universal love. Is that a code word for orgies?"

"It's a code word for celibacy. Celibacy is very big now.

Henry says he never has sex, and he's in a state of perpetual low-level orgasm from meditating, chanting and giving out love to everyone. It's just my luck to meet a man like that." Alexandra cleared her throat. "He couldn't spend a lot of time with me at Nirvana. There were ten other women he had to keep happy. They followed him around like baby ducks following their mother. He said I could be with him all day long if I'd join the others, but I couldn't. They were fat. One of them had green hair. It felt humiliating to me. I made him come to my room to see me.

"While he was sitting there talking about the bliss beyond passion, I was getting undressed. He watched me; he didn't even smile. Women must be getting undressed in front of him all the time. He said, 'You have a beautiful body, Alexandra. I think I'll celebrate it by just sitting here with you.' I got down on my knees in front of him. He patted my head, the way you pat a dog's head.

"I'm a little ashamed of this part. I was very angry. I said, 'Get out of here, you cocksucker.'

"He said, 'All right, Alexandra. You can stay in your room and rest. Celebrate yourself if you want to. I'll see you later at my talk."

Helena stopped winding and put the ball of wool down in her lap. "Celebrate yourself! That's disgusting," she said. "I know what he meant by that."

Alexandra said, "I wasn't feeling sexy anymore. I have to feel wanted to feel sexy. So I lay down on my bed and kicked and screamed until I fell asleep. When I woke up I realized I had no reason to be angry with him. He'd never led me on or laid a finger on me. That girl's green hair was just an excuse so I could keep fantasizing about him and me alone together. I like green hair, if it's a nice, pale green. I'm getting to like magenta, too. So that was that. Henry and I are as close as ever. It's as if the whole thing never happened."

"I think he's very strange," said Helena. "You can't just go around giving out love to everyone or they'll all expect to be taken care of for the rest of their lives."

"He came over yesterday while Anne-Marie was here cleaning," Alexandra said. "You should have seen him flirt with her. At least I thought it was flirting. He said it was the way you gave universal love to an island girl. I would feel better about it if I hadn't caught him doing it behind my back. I was in the kitchen making herb tea. All of a sudden I heard her giggling in the living room. I heard her say, 'Oh, go on, Mr. Henry,' as if she were the old family retainer and he'd been courting me for twenty years. But she and I are still on a trial basis.

"When I went into the living room, there he was standing behind her, pulling her hair back from her face and showing her what she looked like in the mirror. She looked transformed—as if someone had just made love to her. He couldn't have made love to her, though. They hadn't been out of my sight more than three minutes. He told me later he'd just stood in the room with her and opened himself up. I don't know why I can't do that with people. I do love him, you know. He's probably more evolved than the rest of us; that's why he seems strange to you."

Helena liked to think she had no prejudices where her friends were concerned. "Okay," she said, "I'm having a house party at Salt Lick, my mother's place on Long Island, weekend after next. Come and bring him if you want to. I'll give you a room with twin beds."

"I don't know. I think I want to phase Henry out a little and maybe phase Giorgio back in a little," said Alexandra, in the sober tone of someone making a grave decision.

"You'll be able to see Giorgio all you like. Kitty's bring-ing him."

"Henry smiles all the time. He might spook some of the men."

"I'm sure John will smile back at him," said Helena.

Alexandra said, "Okay. I'll ask him."

Helena hung up, finished her ball of wool, put it in a big shopping bag and went to her back window. On the ledge of the next apartment building, a floor below, the pigeons were cooing to their young. Pigeons, who seemed completely ab-sorbed in their business out on the street, made noises at home that indicated a luxurious pleasure. Was it the com-fort of the nest itself, or the presence of the young (never seen on the street) that forced these rapturous sounds from their throats? A barren woman could get to hate herself, studying the domestic life of pigeons.

She thought of her mother, cooing over her new baby, nurse Flora James. Writers, painters and composers consid-ered the things they made to be children of a sort, and were perfectly willing to give them up for money.

Actually, she was looking forward to the two days and nights with Violet, Kitty, Alexandra and their men as a way to put some air between John and her. Maybe they'd been concentrating too much on one subject with each other. If there was something ungenerous about a woman who couldn't get pregnant, there was something ridiculous about a man who couldn't inspire his woman to conceive. In that regard, she wished John hadn't been made an honorary fire fighter last week. There wasn't a woman she could think of who'd be aroused to passion by a portly, middle-aged man in an honorary fire fighter's hat.

EIGHT

The minute she got home after her elevator episode and calmed down the dog, Kitty called Violet. "I've overextended myself," she said. "I'm expanding my business, I've got Giorgio to worry about, and a dog I can't housebreak. There's a leak in my bathroom ceiling. The superintendent's just been fired for trying to rape one of the girls downstairs. Didn't he know they were lesbians, for Christ's sake? Judy Thaxter, the *Gossip* reporter, follows me everywhere I go. Her lipstick and eyeliner are always smeared and I don't know whether I should offer her a makeup lesson. Just now I got stuck in a crowded elevator for a half hour. I freaked out. I shouldn't ever leave the store during business hours. Judy was right beside me, taking notes."

"She took notes while I was fighting with Philip at your

party," Violet said. "Her photographer took pictures. She wouldn't use any of that, would she?"

Kitty took off her green lizard shoes and stretched her legs out on her white sofa. "Probably not," she said.

"We're getting along so well now. I hate to think about how awful I used to be."

"You can explain that to them if they ever do a story on you."

"Don't be bitchy. I was just sharing my experience with you of how relationships can improve."

"I've had a terrible day," Kitty said. "I was late for an appointment with my accountant. I don't know why I invited Judy along. She said she wanted to see me on other people's turf. I don't like other people's turf; that's why I have my own business. The truth is, I may need her to do me a favor later on, if she turns up any embarrassing information. All this manipulation is giving me stress headaches."

"It's only unsuccessful manipulation that gives people stress headaches," Violet said.

"I'm trying to tell you," Kitty said, "I freaked out in an elevator in the American Dynamic Appearances Building."

"Poor you," Violet said at last. "Is there anything I can do?"

"Please listen to me. That's all."

"You just said you freaked out in that gorgeous new pink and green building on Madison. Tell me what that's like inside, if it's not too insensitive to ask. Philip says sometimes I'm insensitive."

The trick was to get Violet interested in your story before she thought of another way to turn the conversation to herself. "I'll tell you about the inside of the elevator," Kitty said. "It's pale peach molded plastic with peach carpeted floors. There's warm yellow light radiating from a big disk on the ceiling. The elevator corners are curved, and the doors fit together so you can't see a seam. It's very snug for a short ride, but when you're stuck it's like being inside a peach plastic Tampax holder. Not only that, there's Musak. Musak brings out my latent hostility. I said to Judy, 'If they don't turn that off I'm going to make trouble.'

"Judy nodded and wrote it down in her notebook.

"I realized I'd have to take matters into my own hands. I said out loud, in my sweetest voice, 'Let's take a vote. Is there anyone in this elevator who's going to get violent if the Musak is turned off? Because I'm going to get violent if it's not.'

"The man who'd called the starters to tell them we'd stopped called again and said we needed the Musak turned off. They told him they couldn't. He said, 'We have a very nervous woman in a very crowded elevator here.' It's amazing the ideas people get. I have nerves of steel."

"I was stuck in an elevator once all by myself," Violet said. "I rang the emergency bell for ten minutes before they rescued me. They came in through the ceiling wearing huge rubber boots. It was like the beginning of a porno movie."

Kitty pulled her knees up to her chest and huddled herself into her corner of the sofa. Someone seemed to be driving an elevator alarm past her windows. Unless it was a new kind of police siren. "I'm not very good in unfamiliar situations," she said. "I thought all the other passengers were acting too calm. Almost as if they'd been drugged. It's not natural to be calm when you're in body contact with a lot of strangers and you're suspended by cables in a peach plastic Tampax holder thirty-two floors off the ground. You can't do any of the things you normally would to relieve the tension. You can't lean against the person next to you, or cry, or sing, or have sex with anyone."

"You shouldn't sing," Violet said. "Your voice doesn't do you justice, really."

"The polite thing to do in an elevator is remain silent, facing front, as if no one else were there. And that's what everyone was doing. I was, too. My nose was practically pressing the button for the fourteenth floor. I could smell sweaty wool. Ooooh." Kitty shook her head and shoulders as if the smell were still with her. "I might as well have been ten years old again. When I was really bad my father used to lock me in the closet. I would get into a corner and crouch there. I felt as if the heavy coats were crushing me. The smell of sweaty wool still makes me want to pass out.

"So I started to talk. I said, 'That's modern life. They build a big, tall, pink and green building, you get inside of it, and you're trapped. A lot of other people are trapped with you, so you're scared to death but you have to be considerate. Pretty soon human smells begin to nauseate you. You hope you're not offending anyone. How can you help it? This city is just too crowded.'

"A woman near the back of the car said, 'My boss is never going to believe this.' Everyone laughed.

"I said, 'It's no wonder people act peculiar in this city. There's too much movement. Can you imagine how strange it would look to someone who died just fifty years ago? There are people traveling up, down and sideways, people in cars and buses and subways, people walking and people on bicycles, all rushing to get somewhere. Then there are people in shorts and canvas shoes with stripes on them running around and around the block. And there are other people asking the runners questions, even though it's obvious they're participating in a sport. No one would get on a basketball court and ask someone the way to Madison Avenue. Do they think people who wear shorts and run around on the sidewalks deserve to be punished for showing their legs? This is a terribly Puritan country.' "

Aphrodisia jumped up on the sofa next to Kitty, cocked her bony head and looked at her mistress with soft, dark eyes. Their expression, if she had been human, would have been compassionate. "Good girl," Kitty said. Aphrodisia nodded. Kitty said, "Everyone was facing in my direction, probably because I was at the front of the car. That was fine with me. I had a lot to say. It was as if someone had pulled a switch in my brain. All the indignities I've suffered in New York all these years, all the meannesses and rudenesses I try not to notice because I believe a good mood means good business, all the little incidents I never think about suddenly seemed to be the only things that mattered.

"I said, 'Recently I was given a dog. I walk her twice a day, and I clean up after her though it makes me feel ridiculous.

" 'My dog is a very thin breed, and so I get criticism from the sidewalk. "Hey, lady, why don't you feed your dog," they say. I say, if you're not a dog owner you don't talk to me about my dog. I never say to the people who make fun of my dog, "Hey, sonny, you could use a change of underwear," though I'm sure all of them could or they wouldn't be scratching themselves. I don't go outside to pass judgments on my neighbors. I suppose those boys don't live in my neighborhood, but that's beside the point, they're on my street.'

"A man's voice from behind me said, 'You sound like an elitist snob to me.'

"A woman near him said, 'It's not easy for a woman to

walk around in this city. It's full of people who want to write their names on everything.'

"A woman on the other side said, 'I don't think anybody cares that we're stuck up here,' and she started to cry.

"I thought, at least I'm not the one who cried, but I was in danger of losing the floor. I knew if I stopped talking I'd do something embarrassing."

Violet said, "I would have been embarrassed to be giving a speech."

"I thought of it as having my say," Kitty said. "But I was beginning to run out of pet peeves. I wanted to give them a few minutes on people who won't stand to the right on an escalator so you can walk past them on the left, and cab-drivers who won't listen to directions and restaurants where they take your plate away while the person you're eating with is still eating. I didn't know what I'd do after that. My feet were killing me."

"I'm thinking of getting some lower-heeled shoes for the office," Violet said.

"The taller I feel, the better I feel. I wish I felt better now." Kitty curled her toes as tight as she could, sending waves of pent-up energy through her legs. "Just in time, the elevator gave a little shudder and we zoomed downstairs," she said. "When we hit ground I said, 'Thank you all for listening to me.'

"A woman right near me said, 'You did a good job, honey.'

"I didn't realize how wound up I was until I ran into Henry Sweet."

"You didn't tell me about Henry Sweet," Violet said, as if she would have been paying more attention all along if she'd known there'd be a man in the story.

"Judy and I were in the lobby looking for a phone booth, to call my accountant and tell him I wasn't coming up after all. I saw Henry's big, solid body shimmering in front of me like a mirage. I practically threw myself into his arms and I started to cry. Judy said she had to leave. I'll bet she went running back to her office to type up a new lead for her story. Henry took me into the atrium."

"Henry Sweet. He seems awfully blah, but maybe I ought to get to know him," Violet said.

"Forget it," Kitty said. "He's asexual."

Violet said, "I just said I ought to get to know him, the same way you and Alexandra have gotten to know him."

"You have to be willing to listen to a lot of strange advice from Henry," Kitty said. "Like he said if I wanted to stop feeling crowded in a tight spot, I could open myself up inside and pretend other people are part of me. How do you do that?"

"I can only do it when I'm having sex," Violet said.

"Not everything is sex, you know."

"What's wrong with you?"

"Henry said what I did in the elevator probably saved me from a real nervous breakdown. He said he thinks I've been putting too much positive energy into negative channels and that's been blocking my flow of love." Kitty yawned, shook herself and stretched her legs out, pushing the dog off the sofa.

"It sounds as if you have Alexandra's disease," Violet said.

"Alexandra doesn't have any common sense," Kitty said. "She thinks life has to be perfect or it's not worth her while to participate. Life is never perfect."

"Are you two fighting?"

"When I invited Giorgio to Helena's mother's for the weekend he asked me whether Alexandra would be there. So I'd like to kill her, that's all."

"Oh, don't worry," Violet said. "He must have been wondering if there would be any food restrictions. When I told Philip she was coming that's the first thing he wanted to know."

Kitty decided not to get angry at Violet for first arousing her suspicions about Alexandra and then making them seem silly. "Maybe that's it," she said. "Giorgio was really thinking about food. My mother used to say I jumped to conclusions too fast. I'd see her with a skirt on and figure she was going to town and leaving me to mind the kids and the chickens. I'd hear her using the cleaver in the kitchen and assume we were having fried chicken for dinner. Usually I was right, but Miss Know-It-All never asks questions, so she doesn't learn anything new."

"Was this your real mother or the one you invented?" Violet said.

"It was my mother." The hairs on Kitty's arms stood up. She felt like a dog who's just got a scent of rabbit. "When did I tell you about inventing her?" she said.

"Oops," said Violet. "I don't remember. It must have been when we were talking about how our parents make us up."

"We never had that conversation."

"We didn't? Then how did I know about your mother?"

Kitty said, "Okay, just tell me who else you told."

"I haven't told anybody. Why don't you ask Helena who else she told? She told me. I know it's a secret. I thought I could tell you, since you already knew."

"That's true. I did already know." Kitty wished she could throttle Helena and cut out Violet's tongue. "I hope you haven't told anybody and I know you won't, because it's really important that you don't," she said. "It's just like you wouldn't like me to tell anyone about your affair with Roger."

"Roger," Violet said. "Sometimes I think I must be crazy. I'm sleeping with a movie star but I'm not getting any of the side benefits. Did you see his picture in the *Post* with Jennifer Charmant at that party for the opening of Jail?"

Kitty said, "Don't worry. That place won't last. The gimmick is wrong. It's just an old police station. All the help are dressed in police uniforms. So you're having a nice conversation with someone, and suddenly this cop is standing next to you eavesdropping. He says he wants to take your drink order, but you don't want to tell him what you drink. You don't really want to check your coat with a cop, either. You're afraid to do drugs anywhere on the premises. It's not much fun."

"He told me he was taking Jennifer out just to be seen in public," Violet said. "But I wish I didn't know about it. I almost like it better when he's in California. Except then he phones me every day. Freddy wants to know when he's going to sign with us. Roger's just making his daily obscene phone call."

"Oh, yeah?" Kitty said. "Lucky you."

Violet said, "It's excruciating. I keep worrying Freddy's going to come in and catch me. After one of those calls I'm like a lightbulb that's been screwed into a socket for too long. I mean hot. Sometimes I call Philip at the lab to relieve the tension. He's very sweet. He says I can't keep calling him there, but I can tell he loves it. Why shouldn't he? Most of the time he doesn't do anything but cut up genes and paste them back together."

"I love desire," Kitty said. "Who do you suppose phones Roger to put him in the mood to phone you?"

"I don't think it's that way at all," said Violet. "I think Roger wakes up with a hard-on. When we hang up he masturbates."

Kitty really didn't want to talk about sex. "At least now that you're seeing Roger you don't complain about Philip anymore," she said.

"They're different problems," Violet said. "Philip and I are getting along like whipped butter and hot toast, now that I've started telling him what I want. He likes to listen to me; he even likes to cook for me. If only I didn't need someone to be angry at, I could kick Roger out and Philip and I could settle down."

"Why don't you settle down with Philip and take up tennis?"

"I have trouble keeping my eye on the ball," Violet said.

Kitty thought of Giorgio in his tennis whites. She thought of his tender pink and green cock resting on its sweet balls. Why was Giorgio in Chicago tonight, when she really needed him? She felt as if she'd been talking for hours and it hadn't helped. "I'm going to get undressed and walk the dog," she said. "If you don't hear from me in the next three days, it means we've been sexually assaulted."

First Alexandra got a busy signal twice at Kitty's number. Then no answer at all. She wasn't exactly comfortable, anyway, putting a lot of effort into phoning a person she didn't like in order to pump that person about a stolen man. If Kitty was really serious about Giorgio, she'd already decided she would be magnanimous and give him up for good. She would get a gold star in the imaginary book where she entered the things she did to be right instead of happy. That

is, if Kitty answered the phone at all. It was on its fourth
ring, two more to go. This would be Alexandra's last try and
she was looking forward to thinking about what she would
wear tonight, to go to dinner with her agent Harvey Fisher
and see if he couldn't get her more money now that she was
doing monologues and pulling a lot of mail, when Kitty
picked up the receiver. "Did I interrupt something?" Alexandra said.

"I've just come back from walking Aphrodisia. Now
she's on her hind legs trying to lick my face. It's her way of
saying thank you. If I tell her to get down I'll make her feel
bad. Then I'll feel bad because she loves me no matter what
I do."

"That's what everyone's looking for, unconditional
love," Alexandra said. "I don't know if I'd want it from a
dog."

"At least a dog won't give you a dog, and then stand
around smiling when it jumps on you."

Kitty didn't sound to Alexandra like a woman in love.
"I've been sitting here thinking about what wonderful
friends I have, and I realized we haven't talked in ages, darling," she said. "I wanted to find out how you are."

"The *Gossip* reporter has been following me around for
days. I'm exhausted," said Kitty vivaciously.

"I'll bet you'll feel lonely after she's finished with you.
That's what happened to me when *Womankind* wrote about
me three years ago."

"And that was only in a roundup of radio shows and you
only got two paragraphs, right?"

"My ratings went up a whole point." Alexandra wished
Harvey had told her where he was taking her. She didn't
know whether to wear uptown clothes or downtown clothes.
The black and silver 1940s dress would work anywhere

since you could look at it as a beautiful object or a costume, depending on what kind of head you had, but she'd be letting herself in for a night of adjusting shoulder pads.

"I'm trying not to think about what a few pages in *Gossip* will do for my business. I have more than I can handle right now," Kitty said. "What I hope is that the story will help other women who want to succeed. I think attention in the press is an opportunity to give back some of what people have given to you."

You might imagine Kitty would be satisfied enough having Giorgio—if she really had him—so she wouldn't feel she had to lord it over her friends about her very transitory worldly success. "You're lucky it's a one-time thing,' Alexandra said. "No matter how much you give the public, once they know you, they just want more. Then you have to retreat."

"Why retreat? Henry would say it's all just love, wouldn't he?"

Alexandra said, "I think Henry's nerve endings are very deeply buried. He can't feel pain, or fear, or anything intense, so to him all feelings are love—on a very mild, platonic level."

"It might be a challenge to make someone like that wake up."

"You know what? I'm getting tired of challenges." Alexandra yawned. "I want a man who adores me."

"I get bored if I'm not stimulated," Kitty said.

"Then you're lucky to have a stimulating man like Giorgio."

Kitty said, "You said he never listened to you."

"Did I? That must have been right before I went on my fast. I was so bummed out. I felt as if I were broadcasting at full volume and everyone was tuned in to another station. I

found out it was my own channels that were blocked. I'm
like a different person now. You know, the night Giorgio fell
for you I didn't even notice?"

"You either like Italian men or you don't," Kitty said.

Alexandra said, "Has he invited you to Milano to meet
his mama?"

"I'll be lucky to get as far as Long Island for Helena's
weekend," Kitty said. "I've never been so busy in my life.
Anyway, as far as Italian cities go, I'd rather be in Venice,
wouldn't you?"

Poor Kitty. If she were as good at love as she apparently
was at business, she would have been married to some gorgeous millionaire long ago. "Don't overwork yourself,"
Alexandra said.

"At least when I'm working I always know what I'm
doing," said Kitty.

When Alexandra hung up she sat back in her chair. She
didn't know what to think about Giorgio, or her future, so
she hugged herself and tried to make her mind go blank.
Immediately the new gray Japanese dress with the strange
ties under the bosom and the strange bumps on the skirt
came into her head. It was perfect. It looked funky and
glamorous at the same time—insofar as any piece of cloth-
ing that cost over three hundred dollars could still be called
funky. She'd see whether it needed ironing and then she'd
try to make her mind go blank. If she was ever going to
trust herself, she had to learn to love the blank part of her
mind.

Kitty went straight from the phone to the English rose-
wood secretary in the living room where she picked up her
galleys of *Tasting,* a book about food. The author, a steady
customer, wanted a quote for the dust jacket. Satisfied that

she still had more work than she could possibly do, she let her thoughts wander. Immediately she was back in the peach plastic elevator. The lights were on her. She'd run out of things to say and was singing "Nearer My God to Thee." All the other passengers held their hands to their ears. Their faces looked pained, as if she were spewing poison gas at them. It occurred to her she could probably benefit from a fasting cure.

NINE

Kitty and Violet were the first to talk to each other about it after Helena's weekend. Kitty called Violet on Monday morning while she was taking her chamomile tea break. "My head aches behind my eyes," she said. "It's been this way since last night. I think I have a brain tumor."

"Philip and I spent last night putting Rita on a train back to school," Violet said.

In Kitty's opinion, a young woman who practically refused to speak and still got men more than twice her age to take her rowing at all hours knew enough to put herself on a train back to school. "Rita's grown up since the last time I saw her," she said.

Violet said, "She thinks it's my fault she's unhappy. But I've done the best I could. She was the one who wanted to go away to school. She said she needed to be with her peers to find out what was normal and what wasn't. Is it my fault her roommate stopped talking to her? We're lucky Helena had room for her this weekend."

"So she was unhappy this weekend," Kitty said. "That doesn't mean she's unhappy."

"If she wasn't unhappy, why would she want me to be unhappy? She says there isn't room in my apartment for three adults. Now that she's a sophomore in high school she thinks she's an adult."

"You mean she doesn't want Philip around?"

"It's okay if we do things together, but she doesn't approve of illicit sex."

On the whole Kitty thought people who had children got what they deserved. "Don't worry, Violet," she said to be supportive. "You can take care of yourself."

"I almost killed Helena this weekend, if that's what you mean," Violet said. "What made her think she had to invite Roger in, just because he showed up at her door? And John didn't have to ask him to spend the night. I think he did it out of meanness."

"He probably didn't know about you and Roger," Kitty said. "Helena says he's not interested in her friends' affairs."

"Then why does he always make a pass at me when he gets me alone?"

"Maybe it's the way you flirt with him."

Violet said, "That's blame-the-victim mentality. He always seems starved for affection. Which reminds me. I got her machine this morning. Only Helena could leave the house just when she knows all her friends are dying to talk to her."

"I left a message," Kitty said. "Maybe she had an errand."

"She has all day to do her errands. But anyway, I was talking about Roger. It's a good thing I told Philip about him. I don't mean I told him. I said he was a drunk and a womanizer, and Freddy wanted me to woo him as a client. So when he grabbed me and called me his wench, Philip wasn't surprised. Of course I had to give Philip a lot of extra attention to make up for it.

"As soon as I got Roger alone I said, 'I don't know what you're doing here, but I'm here with my daughter and the man I may want to marry, and if you spoil it for me I'll see that you never work in pictures again.'

"Roger looked at me as if I'd said something very witty. We were standing in the dining room staring out at the lake and smiling at each other. Anyone who saw us might have thought we were talking about boating conditions. Roger said, 'Just come to my room before dinner and jerk me off. I promise I won't tell anybody.'

"I said, 'Are you crazy? I could be caught.'

"He said, 'Okay, just come to my room and watch me jerk myself off.' What makes men think women like to watch them jerk off?" Violet said the words "jerk off" as if they had quotes around them.

"Some women do." Kitty's head throbbed.

Violet said, "I told him I'd meet him in the garden at six, but only to talk about the terms of his contract with Star-Time.

"Just then Helena sidled over and said she wanted to show him around the property. When he smiled at her she blushed, the little flirt."

"God will punish you for being greedy," said Kitty, who liked contemplating Violet's appetites.

"You're right," Violet said. "Helena probably saved my life. I ought to get her a present. When I went to the garden at six and Roger wasn't there, I should have been thankful he was still with Helena."

Kitty said, "I think Helena's hot for Roger."

"Don't be silly," Violet said. "Helena doesn't get hot. She's afraid of sex."

"Even I'm afraid of sex sometimes." Kitty took a soothing sip of flowery chamomile. "It gets in the way. It's like a drug. You have too much of it and you forget that other things are more important."

Violet said, "Am I wrong, or did you give Alexandra your dog?"

Kitty sat up straight, relaxed her shoulders and thought of the face of the *Mona Lisa,* a vision that brought a smile to her lips in the most uncomfortable situations. "Aphrodisia attached herself to Alexandra," she said. "Followed her everywhere. She must have liked her smell."

"Alexandra doesn't smell."

"All animals have smells. Ask Giorgio. What I'm doing is, I've given her Giorgio first. If she decides to keep him, then I'll throw in Aphrodisia."

Violet said, "Can you hold on for a minute?" and put Kitty on hold. Kitty looked up to see Serge gliding toward her desk in his chic French moccasins, holding a sheaf of papers and a checkbook in his hand. She put the receiver down on the desk and signed ten letters and six checks and took a gulp of chamomile; it went down the wrong pipe, making her cough. When she put the phone back to her ear, Violet was waiting for her. "You don't happen to know any real graffiti artists, do you?" Violet said. "We need some for a party we're giving in the subway yard."

Kitty said in a strained voice, "I'm ready to write on the walls myself. Judy Thaxter is doing her last interview with me this afternoon. Then I may take a vacation."

Violet skipped a beat, as if to distance herself from any possible emotional outburst on Kitty's part. "Are you upset?" she said. "I'd love to talk about it but I can't stay on the phone much longer or Freddy will kill me."

"I'm not upset," Kitty said. "I'm exhausted. I think this diet is making me weak."

"Why are you on a diet?"

"I told you at breakfast Saturday morning."

"You did? I must have been watching Rita slop her cereal on the table. I pay The Moated Grange a lot of money to teach her table manners."

"Was she wearing anything under that little bathrobe, by the way?" Kitty said. "Giorgio wanted to know. That was before he got a look at Alexandra in her morning kimono."

"Let's not talk about Rita," Violet said. "I want to know about your diet."

"I eat brown rice, beans, seaweed and orange vegetables. Henry gave it to me. I've been feeling jumpy ever since I got stuck in that elevator. I told him I dream of my parents' clothes closet. Aphrodisia smells like sweaty wool. I'm afraid things are closing in on me. He said it would be a good idea if I purified my life.

"I could lose a lot of business if anyone knew I wasn't eating my own food. So I waited for the weekend to start, when I could be among friends. I tipped the cook to soak the beans and boil everything up for me."

"Beans. It sounds very boring," Violet said.

"I almost went off it when I got sick Saturday night. But Henry was insistent. He said if this diet didn't make you sick, it couldn't make you well." Kitty put her right arm around her stomach, which felt sore to the touch.

"That's why you weren't at dinner Saturday night," Violet said. "I got to the table late."

"He could have told me what to expect before I did it," Kitty said. "Everyone must have thought I was sick because of the treasure hunt."

"I don't know how Helena could have paired up Alexandra and Giorgio," Violet said.

"I think it was just bad timing." Aphrodisia's image flashed into Kitty's head. The dog was galloping toward her at thirty-five miles an hour, carrying Alexandra's purple underpants in her mouth. "Of course," she said, "for its entertainment value, I suppose the timing was pretty good."

"You sound bitter."

Kitty said, "I'm not bitter, it's this tea that's bitter. I have to go get some honey for it." She hung up, picked up the tea cup with its saucer and smashed them on her black tile floor. Sometimes she thought no one had the same delicacy of feeling that she had. She rang Serge. "They overdid the polish on my desk," she said. "My Chinese tea cup just slid off and smashed to bits on the floor."

Helena saw John go off to work on Monday morning with a mixture of tenderness and relief. She felt closer to him than she had in months after their weekend with her friends, and yet she couldn't very well tell him the things that were on her mind. She couldn't tell any of her friends, either. Kitty or Alexandra would feel bad not to have phoned to thank her first. Violet wouldn't care, but she didn't want to talk to Violet just yet. As soon as John left she turned on the phone machine to screen her calls, making herself feel superfluous.

So on a morning when she might have lain in bed accepting gratitude from the people she liked best, Helena became an early customer at Smith's. There, on the upper floors, she studied all the model rooms even though they were featuring driftwood, bought new linens for every bed in Salt Lick, and had late-morning tea at the Plummerie. In this last occupation she was periodically interrupted by visions of the bright blue eyes of Roger Rathbone. Roger was gazing up at her from his kneeling position at her feet, while she sat shivering with desire in the room she still thought of as her father's study, in her father's favorite red leather wing chair.

As soon as she got home and got her messages she settled down on her bed with her knitting on her lap and phoned Kitty. "I told you I didn't like Scarlett Atwill's handshake," she said. "I just saw her at Smith's, arm in arm with a very attractive man. She claimed he was her interior designer."

"Oh, that's the man Larry imported from Virginia to do their Southern mansion. His name is Jefferson."

"Jefferson. Haha," Helena said.

"Scarlett's so much younger than Larry, he knows he can't keep up with her every minute. He wants to make sure she enjoys herself," Kitty said.

Helena said, "But that's shocking. I'm younger than John. Not that much younger of course, but I don't know what I'll do if he's starting to fall behind."

"You don't have anything to worry about," Kitty said.

Helena couldn't stand Kitty's knowing tone. "Then how come I almost went to bed with Roger Rathbone?" she said, and she began knitting, click, click, click.

"Roger's a terrible flirt," Kitty said. "Hold on while I tell Serge to pretend I've gone to lunch. Later I'll have a bowl of brown rice and yams at my desk."

Helena finished a row of purl and put her knitting down so she could think about what she was saying. "I'm glad you didn't notice the way Roger was looking at me," she said when Kitty got back on the line. "I was afraid my husband would see. I almost fainted when Roger drove up to the house in his green Jaguar. I'd just had a dream the night before about him driving up to the house. His car was red, though."

"That's very interesting," Kitty said.

"It's not interesting that I dreamed about him. He's in a lot of my dreams. He's always looking into my eyes and asking me to run away with him. So I was afraid that was what he was actually there for. Then I saw he was wearing those awful mirror shades. He needed a shave, too. He looked as if he'd slept in his car. In any case, John was standing right next to me on the porch, practically panting. He'd never admit it, but Roger is his favorite movie star. Roger said Violet was expecting him for a business conference."

"Violet says he followed her out."

"Do you believe that?"

"It's possible."

"I don't believe it," said Helena. "Roger's story made perfect sense to me. That's why I invited him in. When we shook hands I could feel the heat coming off his body. Before I knew it, John had asked him to stay the night.

"Violet pulled me aside and whispered, 'I didn't know he was coming. I'll die if he ruins things for Philip and me.' Then she dragged Roger off to the dining room, to give him a drink."

"Didn't Roger grab Violet and call her his wench right in front of Philip?"

Helena had no memories of Roger showing affection for Violet. "Does Violet say so?" she said. "I didn't see that. I was very angry with her for arranging a tryst at my mother's house. What did she expect me to do with Philip and Rita if she disappeared? I went to the kitchen to tell Mathilda we had one more for dinner, and I knocked over a big pot and spilled water and beans on the floor. I was in a state. I was afraid of Roger because he's so attractive. But then I thought, what if I'm meant to leave John for Roger? What's he doing in my dreams? So I found Roger and Violet in the dining room and I offered to show him around. You should have seen the look Violet gave me. It made up for hours of listening to her talk about men. She could hardly complain that I was taking Roger off her hands. The whole situation was thrilling. It made me feel a little sick.

"I took Roger to the garden. He started right off standing too close. I wanted him to know who I was, first, so I told him the way I feel about design."

"He probably hadn't even had breakfast," Kitty said.

"I think people who don't care about design are shallow." Helena scanned her bedroom, with its sleek pieces of 1930s Moderne in pale polished woods, and smiled with pleasure at her own good taste. "Roger just wasn't concentrating," she said. "While I was pointing out the design of the potato field he said, 'You know, you're very beautiful.'

"I told him he ought to save that kind of talk for Violet.

"He said, 'Violet likes to play dangerous games. I'm just a country boy.'"

"A country boy! What a laugh," Kitty said.

"He said, 'Your purity is exciting to me.'"

"He was really laying it on thick."

"That's what I thought," Helena said. You couldn't expect Kitty to believe a movie star could have fallen in love with one of her best friends when she herself had just been jilted by an overly friendly Italian playboy. "But men don't usually ask you to marry them when they're just flirting, do they?"

"It's too bad you're already married," Kitty said.

Helena pretended she hadn't heard her. "We were in Fish for Compliments. Did I tell you he insisted on doing the shopping with me? We were looking at the lobsters nudging each other around the bottom of the tank. I was thinking about how strange it must be to live in the water, inside a shell, with bug eyes on the sides of your head. Roger said, 'How I yearn for the stillness of domestic life. I only exist on soundstages, and in bars, hotels and the first-class compartments of airplanes.' He grabbed my hand and looked into my eyes, and his eyes were really bright. My skin actually started to tingle. He said, 'I think I could be happy with you, Helaine.' "

"Helaine," Kitty said.

"I said, 'It's Helena.'

"He said, 'Let me call you darling.'

"I couldn't help it, my back went up. I said, 'We don't know each other well enough.' I think it's really disrespectful to use terms of endearment with people you hardly know. I wish he didn't have such a gorgeous smile." Helena felt like pulling loops of wool through each other with needles. Life's little routines were such a comfort. She picked up her knitting. "Luckily I had to organize the treasure hunt when we finished shopping," she said, "because Roger wanted me to come to his room."

"Speaking of the treasure hunt, maybe you could tell me how come you put Alexandra and Giorgio on the same team," Kitty said.

Though she tried to concentrate on her knitting, Helena felt the heat of embarrassment spreading through her upper body. She didn't think a really tactful guest would remind the hostess of her lapses, even after the party was over. "I just thought they were old friends," she said, and she added, to show she had no hard feelings, "Poor Kitty."

Kitty said, "Henry says there's a lesson in it for me. But I don't get it yet. I'm seeing Henry tonight."

Helena pictured Henry's horn-rimmed glasses and the faraway look behind them that made her want to shake him. "I'm glad you're not upset about Giorgio," she said.

"I am."

"Then I'm sorry it happened at Salt Lick."

"It was a terrific weekend," Kitty said, "even though I didn't especially enjoy it."

"Did you have fun with John during the treasure hunt? I put him with you because I thought he might want a sympathetic ear. Did he seem a little restless?"

"When my dog arrived in the garden carrying Alexandra's underpants in her mouth, John said, 'My dear, don't be upset, here's an offering from someone who adores you.' "

"Someone who adores you. He must have meant the dog," Helena said.

"If I'd had the presence of mind I could have pretended they were my underpants," Kitty said. "Except that everyone knows I don't wear underpants."

Helena was sorry she'd brought up the treasure hunt. "Philip and I were a team. We discussed Violet," she said. "He said the reason she sometimes behaved badly was she didn't think she was worthy of the responsibilities she'd taken on, being a mother and also shepherding other people's careers. He said, 'A man has to understand a woman like Violet.' "

"Some women have all the luck," said Kitty.

"John took Rita rowing after the treasure hunt. She'd been hanging around him all weekend. On my way to Roger's room I thought of sweet John in the rowboat, putting up with Rita's bad temper, and I felt awful."

"You didn't tell me you went to Roger's room."

Helena curled up against her pillows, trying to remember how awful she felt, on John's account, on her way to visit Roger, but it was her excitement that came back to her. "I thought it would be okay," she said. "It's the room that used to be my father's study. The beds are leather sofas during the day. So there's nothing sexy about it, unless you think maps and books are sexy."

"I do," said Kitty wistfully.

Helena said, "Maybe you're right. Roger was waiting for me with a bottle of champagne. He had on a green velvet smoking jacket. I think he keeps it in the trunk of his car. His eyes looked practically turquoise. I could hardly look at them. I couldn't really look away, either. There was heat coming off his body, the way there was when we first met."

"It must be the way he metabolizes alcohol," Kitty said.

"I took a few sips of champagne," Helena said, "and sat down in my father's red leather wing chair. My face was burning. I felt really sick. I thought, 'This may be it.' Roger sat down on the arm of the chair. We were as close as you can be without touching. Roger said, 'I want you, Helaine.'

"I said, 'It's Helena.' You'd think if he really wanted a woman he'd want to get her name right.

"He said, 'Darling, I bow before you,' and he got off the chair and on to his knees. He actually touched his head to the floor. He said, 'Let me kiss the hem of your skirt.' I was wearing that beautiful old lace wraparound I just bought."

"What a ham," Kitty said.

Helena said, "He's so sexy. He lifted my hem and I could feel it all the way up my legs. When he looked up at me his face was stormy, as if he were having trouble keeping his feelings in control."

"Lust," Kitty said.

"I can only imagine what my face looked like to Henry," said Helena.

"Roger," Kitty said.

"No, Henry." Helena sighed. "Right about then Henry barged into the room carrying his overnight bag. It's probably just as well. I was feeling very strange, almost as if I were a vampire. I was drawn to Roger's neck. I wanted to bend down and bite him."

"You mean you've never bitten a man before?" Kitty said.

Helena knew she should have been glad to find out that other women had desires like hers, but instead this information made her feel very undistinguished. It was a good thing she hadn't told Kitty about the way she'd practically swooned in the wing chair when Roger had merely looked at her, and felt the strangest, sweetest, buzzing, floating feeling when he'd kissed her feet. She said, "When Henry came in I jumped up like a jack-in-the-box. I said, 'I was just plumping up the pillows in here. I'm coming to your room next.'

"Roger hadn't moved from his kneeling position. He said, 'It's a pity you can't stay until I find that earring for you.'

"Meanwhile Henry was looking around the room. There were no pillows. He said, 'The thing is, Alexandra's a little preoccupied right now. I was hoping this room could be my room for the rest of the weekend.'

"I said, 'You're just in time. Roger's serving champagne.' "

Kitty said, "That must have been right after I told Giorgio he was fired. He went straight to Alexandra. I found his behavior nauseating. It was my diet that physically made me throw up."

"I never thought Giorgio was right for you," Helena said sympathetically. "We played a game you would have liked at dinner, too. Everybody had to write down their three favorite animals. It turns out the first animal on your list symbolizes the way you want people to think of you, the second is the way you think of yourself, the third is the way you really are."

"I'm afraid to ask. What was Giorgio, really?" Kitty said.

"Giorgio turned out to be a bull."

"Dumb and stubborn. I'm well out of that," said Kitty.

"Roger was a pig," Helena said.

"Did everybody laugh?"

"Violet laughed. John was a lobster. I've heard they have a highly developed nervous system so they feel everything all over their bodies. I kept thinking, what if someone split him open and grilled him? I wanted to take him under my wing. I was a hen."

"A hen?"

"Violet said, 'You must mean mother hen.' It's true, I do like to see hens sitting on their nests. But Violet had nothing to laugh about. It was her game, and she turned out to be a rabbit. Alexandra was a kangaroo."

"That's perfect," Kitty said. "They're as dizzy as squirrels, only bigger."

"You could say they were unusual and original," Helena said to be fair. "Henry wanted people to think of him as a dolphin. Actually he was a goat."

"A goat? That's great," Kitty said. "Goats love sex."

"He said he chose the goat because people didn't love goats enough. He said the people who chose animals everybody loves, like dogs, cats and horses, were probably too self-centered to have much imagination. He said they wanted to be loved for their personalities, and that was okay, but they ought to know universal love was also available.

"He acts as if he's just giving his opinion and he wants to hear yours; I don't think he cares about your opinion. I said to him, 'Universal love, what's that?'

"He said, 'It's the love people give out when they love themselves enough so they don't need anything in return. Once everybody practices universal love there won't be any more wars.'

"I asked him if he meant going up to people on the street and telling them they're beautiful.

"Philip said, 'I used to do that when I was a hippie.'

"Rita said, '*Beautiful* is just a word hippies used.' Violet gave her a dirty look.

"I hated to agree with Rita. I said, 'I don't think spreading love that way is natural. That's the reason we have manners, so we'll have an acceptable form for expressing our feelings.

"Henry said, 'Feelings should be expressed as they are. Manners get in the way of feelings as they are.' Then he gave an example . . . I hope it's okay to tell you this. He said, 'Why isn't Kitty having dinner with us?'

"I said, 'She's sick. I think it's the seaweed she's eating.'

"He said, 'She says she's sick. I think she feels betrayed. She's sick of the sight of humans. I think a point should have been made to have her at the table. She needs our love right now.'

"I said, 'I think we have to respect her right to be sick of us. Did you try getting her to the table?'

"He said, 'I knocked at her door and called to her. She wouldn't answer.' "

Kitty said, "I was locked in the bathroom throwing up. I didn't hear anyone knocking on the door."

"Exactly what I mean," Helena said. "I said to him, 'Poor Kitty, you probably embarrassed her.'

"He said, 'If she heard me, at least she knows someone cared.'

"I said, 'Do you really care?' I hate people who think manners are a substitute for feelings. They've got it backwards," Helena said.

Kitty said, "Henry just means people shouldn't be uptight about the way they feel."

"Probably you think I'm uptight or I'd be having an affair with Roger Rathbone."

"I think Roger is trouble," Kitty said.

Sometimes Helena didn't understand her friends. Of course Roger was trouble. How else could he make you feel it was up to you to tame him? Not that you'd want a tame Roger, any more than you'd want a John who got too frisky. "John was awfully provocative at dinner," she said. She waited a beat. "I think Rita stirred him up when she made a pass at him in the rowboat."

"No," Kitty said.

"Uh huh. She told him she loved older men because she didn't see enough of her father. She wanted John to be her first."

Kitty said, "She's so beautiful. Do you think John was tempted?"

"No. I think he was stirred up," Helena said. "This is what he said to Henry: 'First of all people can't allow themselves to love other people freely—think of the infidelity that would cause. Second, they can't allow themselves to express their loves freely, or their spouses would find out. It would be the end of marriage and the family as we know it.' "

"John said that?"

"I was terrified. I thought, 'He must suspect something. He must be noticing the looks Roger is giving me. Why can't he just be proud that someone like Roger Rathbone thinks his wife is worth looking at?' I didn't know yet about the rowboat incident.

"Then Henry asked John what was so good about marriage.

"John said the presence of a child, even the potential presence of a child, made marriage sacred. That's what he tells me all the time. He shouldn't say it in public."

Kitty said, "Why not? He doesn't know your friends know about your baby problem."

Helena hated to be put in the wrong. "I don't have a baby problem," she said. "And I'm very happy with my husband. I must be. I prefer him to Roger Rathbone. I made up my mind when Violet dragged Roger off into the garden."

"Violet dragged Roger off?"

"She said they had to talk business; almost everybody there knew better. Poor Philip.

"Roger cast me a glance on his way out the door. I suppose he meant it to say, 'What can I do, I'm trapped in this situation,' but I thought he looked a little pleased with himself. Anyway, for me it was the last straw. I could never take a lover who might betray me in public. Imagine waltzing out into the garden with my best friend in the middle of a dinner party."

"But wouldn't you betray Violet if you had an affair with Roger?"

"I thought about that during dinner. Violet was having a great time, making a show of paying attention to Philip in front of Roger. I thought, I'd hate to see the disappointment in those big brown eyes if Roger and I went off together, but I wouldn't be wrong to do it. That was before I'd decided I didn't want to do it. I don't think a woman can lay claim to more than one man at a time, do you?"

"Do you mean it would have been all right, when you were in the red leather wing chair with Roger, for someone to be fooling around with John?"

"Of course not. He's my husband." If Kitty had ever been married for more than a few minutes when she was eighteen she wouldn't think of relationships in terms of mathematics. "I was just tempted by Roger, that's all. I hope you won't tell Violet what happened, especially since nothing did happen," Helena said.

"I won't tell Violet," said Kitty. "It wouldn't do anyone any good."

Helena felt relaxed and pleased with herself now that she'd told the worst to Kitty. She picked up her knitting and began a row of knit. "The next day Roger and I met in the garden at noon," she said. "It was all over by then. I still felt his body heat but I didn't want to get near him. He said I was afraid my husband would smell him on me.

"I said, 'I suppose you're right.' But I wasn't even thinking of John. It was Mathilda who came into my head, in the kitchen making fish salad, and Ben getting the table set in the dining room. I couldn't remember whether I'd told him to use the glass plates."

"Salads look crisp on glass," Kitty said.

Helena said, "Roger got very dramatic. He said in a stage whisper, 'For once in your life have an adventure. Come away with me.'

"At that moment an adventure was the last thing in the world I wanted. How was everyone else going to spend the rest of the weekend if I came away with him? I said, 'I'm very sorry, but I have other guests.'

"He looked disappointed. I was disappointed, too. The truth is, I've been having fantasies about leaving John for a new life. Of course it was a relief to find out it wasn't another man I wanted."

"But you did want him," Kitty said. "Why didn't you do it?"

Helena saw Roger's blue eyes again. First they mocked her, then they pleaded with her. Then they turned into John's pleading blue eyes. "I don't know how to have a husband and a lover and behave properly," she said. "It would have ruined my marriage."

"It might have strengthened your marriage."

"Even thinking about it strengthened my marriage. Because I realized I could have done it."

"Realizing you could have done it isn't the same thing," Kitty said.

"Maybe not for you. I think I must be very sensitive," Helena said. "Without actually having an affair, I went through all the stages in one weekend: infatuation on Saturday, disillusionment Saturday night and the courage to break it off on Sunday."

"I wonder if Roger's really a good lay," Kitty said.

"If you want to talk about Giorgio now, I'm all ears," Helena said. "But you sound as if you have more interesting things on your mind."

"You mean sex and money," Kitty said. "They're always on my mind."

"Great," Helena said. "Then I'm going to go make some more phone calls."

Alexandra woke up in a bed of rumpled sheets, hugging an exhausted pillow. Giorgio was gone, and it was awfully bright outside. Not gone permanently. He'd left for his place at four in the morning to be there in case his mother phoned.

It was bright like this on Saturday afternoon when she and Giorgio became lovers. When he took her the big knot of pain inside melted like a snowball; it almost made up for the fact that Roger Rathbone didn't remember who she was.

She rolled over, plugged in the phone and called Correct Time. Two-fourteen P.M. and seven seconds exactly. Giorgio would be back for dinner at seven. She wasn't even hungry. She sat up and called Helena. "That was a fabulous weekend," she said, when Helena picked up the phone on the first ring.

Helena said, "I just got off the phone with Kitty. I thought you were going to be Violet. Not that I'm not glad it's you. You certainly surprised everyone this weekend."

"No one was more surprised than I was." Alexandra stretched her legs straight out in front of her. When their toes were pointed they looked almost like a dancer's legs.

"You know Kitty thinks you planned the whole thing," Helena said.

"No one planned it," said Alexandra, who actually thought Fate had planned it. "I didn't know Giorgio and I would be sharing a bathroom. Friday night I was brushing my teeth, wearing an old nightshirt, humming to myself to the rhythm of the toothbrush. Suddenly I heard a door closing and then Giorgio's voice. He said, *'Cara mia.'* He was standing behind me, and he wasn't wearing anything but a brown towel around his waist. I figured he'd come in to take a vitamin pill before he went to work on Kitty. I hadn't seen a naked man in months. Henry was in my room with his maroon and white striped pajamas on. When I came back with my teeth clean he was going to talk to me about renunciation as a way of life.

"I couldn't take my eyes off Giorgio's shoulders. They were creamy tan and as smooth as butterscotch. I forgot to rinse. He said, 'Cara mia, you are so beautiful when you foam at the mouth.' It sounds crazy, but I knew he meant it. When I looked at him again he seemed to have a rosy glow around him. He said, 'Meet me in the garden in fifteen minutes.'

"Just then Kitty started making noises from her room. She said, 'Lover boy, please don't keep Wonder Woman waiting.' "

"Wonder Woman? Really?"

"I told him John was in the garden with Rita, and anyway I'd promised Henry he could teach me to play Go."

"Friday night?" Helena said. "What time was that?"

"About eleven-thirty."

"John said Rita was asking him for career advice."

"That little minx. I thought she wanted to be a botanist," Alexandra said. "How many men do you suppose she's had already?"

"She's supposed to be a virgin," Helena said.

"She's too precocious to be a virgin. I was like her when I was in my twenties. I wanted to have all the men I could so that when I got married I wouldn't feel as if I'd missed anything. The trouble was, I couldn't figure out when I'd had enough. At least I got my appetite back, thanks to Giorgio," Alexandra said.

"I knew it in the bathroom. I wanted him to crush me into the stall shower, turn the water on and rape me standing up. I only restrained myself because of Kitty."

"Not for long." Helena felt more comfortable listening to you once she'd reminded you she was keeping moral tabs. You had to resist the temptation to say things just to shock her. "Oh, I didn't feel I should stay away from him because he belonged to her," Alexandra said. "After all, I had him first. I just don't think it's right to take a man from a friend of yours when she's in bed waiting to be fucked. No matter how much you hate her."

"But you were doing nothing but complaining about Giorgio when Kitty took him. You said you didn't want him."

"Now I'll bet she says she didn't want him, too," Alexandra said. "I may have complained about him but I was still considering him. Every single woman is always considering every man she knows."

"So you think it's perfectly all right for a woman to betray her woman friends?"

"It's not all right, darling, but she can't help betraying them all the time," said Alexandra.

"Then why do you hate Kitty?"

"I don't really hate her anymore. I still think she's a show-off."

Helena said, "She had beans in pots all over the kitchen this weekend. They made Mathilda feel bad. Nothing but beans to eat all through her poor childhood, and now there are rich Americans using them to punish themselves. People shouldn't start new diets on weekends they're invited away. Kitty did the right thing bringing her own food, but even so it made me uncomfortable not to be able to serve her. That's the way I am. I love choosing books and flowers for every room, and planning menus and activities. A hostess wants to be responsible for her guests' happiness."

"Then let me thank you for putting Giorgio and me on the same team for the treasure hunt." Alexandra touched the tender spot where on Saturday afternoon a stone had pressed into her buttocks while Giorgio pounded at her from above.

"I had to apologize to Kitty," Helena said. "I didn't know you wanted to get lost together."

"We went into the potato field to do what the instructions said: 'Make the earth smooth under the trees, find a gold potato and you'll win with ease.' After we'd smoothed the earth under the first tree we sat down to test it. I don't know about you, darling, but I love an earthy man. I just couldn't get up," Alexandra said. "No one would have missed us if that ridiculous dog hadn't found my underpants. It's funny, isn't it, the way animals are projections of their owners."

"Do you think Kitty suspected?"

"I think she was feeling her own karma."

"What does that mean?"

"Karma is a very beautiful Indian concept. It means you get back what you give."

"Yes, but don't the Indians say karma takes lifetimes to work out?"

Alexandra wished that people who didn't understand advanced ideas wouldn't have opinions about them. "Sometimes it takes lifetimes, sometimes it's instant," she said. "I had a talk with Henry about karma after Kitty kicked Giorgio out of her room and I asked Henry if he'd mind moving in with Roger."

"It was you who asked Henry to go to Roger's room?"

"Do you think that was wrong? I would never do that to a man who was hoping to make it with me, but I didn't think Henry would mind. I knew you'd be glad to have Henry in the room to occupy Roger."

"I was enjoying Roger's company," Helena said.

"I love you," Alexandra said. "You're the perfect hostess. But I know Roger. Out of bed he's a complete egotistical bore. He's lost his looks, too. What were we talking about? Oh, yes. So Saturday before dinner I was coming from the bathroom and there was Giorgio, out in the hall. He was carrying two leather bags, wearing his tennis whites. At the same time Henry was coming out of our room humming a Hindu chant. He had on his yoga whites. Giorgio gave me a soulful look. I found out later he was just changing for tennis when Kitty decided to have it out with him. His eyes were so warm I nearly dissolved. Meanwhile, Henry didn't even notice I was there until he bumped into me. I thought, it's about time I started letting my needs come first. So I took Henry back into the room and I said, 'Listen, I don't think I'm going to live a life of renunciation after all. Giorgio loves me.'

"Henry said, 'I love you, too.'

"I said, 'I know, but Giorgio loves me carnally. Would you mind giving up your bed to him?'

"For a minute all the bounce went out of Henry. It was as if he were a Henry balloon, and someone had stuck a pin into him. I felt awful.

"He started gathering up his things. He said, 'In another life I must have had a palace and a harem. I must have been some lecher. Because in this life I still love women, and they interfere with my calling. So I play the eunuch's role. And whenever I get comfortable in one place I know it's time to move on.' "

"You mean karma is being the way you are?" Helena said.

"Karma is the force that makes you the way you are. Think about Kitty. She's a hunter, isn't she? That's her karma. I like to stay close to the hearth. Giorgio needs a hearth to come home to."

Helena said, "I don't think Henry and Roger got along."

There was no point explaining something to Helena that she didn't want to see. "I don't know if they got along," Alexandra said. "When you fall in love your friends suffer. You feel more love for them than ever, but you don't have time to tell them about it. I haven't had a real talk with Henry since he left the room."

"Every time I saw Henry on Sunday he was with Kitty," said Helena.

"You see what I mean about her karma?" Alexandra said. "Anyway, I just got an idea for a monologue. It's about being a guest. That was the best weekend I ever had."

Violet wasn't the kind of woman who made a fuss over who called whom when she wanted to talk. It had been at least two hours since she'd left a message at Helena's—not that anybody was counting—when she phoned again. "I hope this is the real you," she said. "I hate your machine. I fall asleep waiting for your message to be over so I can leave mine. Why don't you get one with a voice-activated message?"

"I like the way this one looks," Helena said.

"I called to thank you for the weekend." Violet lit a cigarette and inhaled. "Even though I want you to know it wasn't easy for me."

"Your phone message said you had a good time."

"I had a great time. I just wish you hadn't invited Roger in." Violet took a large enough breath of smoke to fill up the space Roger occupied in her consciousness, and blew a forceful smoke plume into the office air. "Maybe it was good he was there," she said. "It made me think about what I was doing. But I wish I hadn't started smoking again."

"Violet, think about it for a minute," Helena said in her

most reasonable voice. "Roger wouldn't have been there if you hadn't told him where it was."

"I wouldn't have told him if I'd known he was going to follow me and you were going to make him your star guest."

Helena said, "You know what a demon hostess I am. Can you see me turning Roger Rathbone away from my door? He looked hungry."

"That's part of his charm." Violet mashed her cigarette out in the Luxury Foods ashtray she'd taken from Kitty's last party. "He told me he wanted to see if I really loved Philip. He's such an actor. What did you do with him all day?"

Helena said, "I took him shopping. I think he's awfully lonely. He wants to get married and settle down just like everybody else."

From Helena's point of view all men were the same as John inside, only their envelopes were different. "Roger isn't like everybody else," Violet said.

"He looked really happy pushing a shopping cart."

"He was acting," Violet said. "Even if he did want to settle down, it wouldn't mean the same thing to him it means to an eligible man like Philip."

"The poor baby."

"The poor baby does it to himself." Violet's throat ached. "On Sunday morning he told me he woke up to the sound of Henry chanting in Sanskrit in his room. Where did Kitty find Henry in the first place? He said Henry told him the chant would clear his karma. Then he said, 'I'd been hoping it would be one of the ladies who'd take pity on me in the middle of the night.' What lady did he mean?" Violet's intercom buzzer buzzed. "Can you hold on for just a minute," she said to Helena. She pressed the "hold" button on her phone and switched to her other line where a yellow light was flashing. It was Freddy calling from the mayor's office, wanting to know how she was coming on the graffiti artists. She told him "Big Risk" and "Cherry Bomb" were stopping by in two hours for a conference. She switched back to Helena. "Do you know any real graffiti artists?" she said. "The mayor is promoting planned graffiti. We're having a party in the subway yard. A group of graffiti artists will decorate a brand-new train."

"How much are you paying?" Helena said.

"We're looking for kids who don't have galleries yet. We're giving them all the food they can eat, and I think they should have citations from the mayor." Violet made a note to herself to ask Freddy to talk to the mayor about citations. "Where was I?" she said. "Breakfast with Roger, right? So I said to him, 'Listen, Roger, I told you I couldn't come near you with Philip in the house.' Philip was out doing his three-mile morning run. It keeps him from getting angry with me during the day. I felt sorry for Roger. He looked pale and weak. I said, 'I wish you hadn't come here. You know I'm nuts about you, but if I have to choose between you and Philip, I choose Philip. I know him better.' "

"He said, 'Are you kicking me out? I wonder if that means my karma is cleared.'

"I'd already gotten him to sign the contract with Star-Time in the garden the night before. I said, 'We can still be together as counselor and client.'

"He said, 'So you won't be the one to sew on my buttons and put my socks in pairs.' "

"He's awfully flip, isn't he?" Helena said. "But I think he has very deep feelings."

"Most of them self-pity," Violet said. "The funny thing

is, when I first told him I'd chosen Philip, I wasn't all that sure what I meant. It was the remark about socks and buttons that really turned me off. Roger's a great lay. He isn't the kind of man a woman wants to pair socks for." Violet's intercom buzzed. "Hold on for just a minute," she said to Helena, and she switched to her other line.

"I've been trying to call you for the past half hour," Kitty said.

"I didn't get any messages."

"I know. I couldn't get near the phone. Why didn't you tell me about the dinner on Saturday night? It sounds as if John practically announced he was having an affair with Rebecca."

"He never mentioned Rebecca."

"Helena told me he said it was natural to love more than one person at a time. Do you think he wants her to find out?"

"I didn't think she even heard him," Violet said.

"She told me she thought he was being provocative."

"Her face was flushed," Violet said. "I thought it was the heat of being the hostess. She's on the other line right now. We're talking about my favorite subjects, Roger and Philip."

"You're terrible," Kitty said. "She just treated you to a weekend in the country."

"Don't worry, I'm going to send her a bread-and-butter letter. Anyway, I don't think she wants to talk about herself."

"Call me if you find out anything," Kitty said.

Violet switched back to Helena. "That was Kitty," she said.

Helena said, "Poor Kitty."

"Kitty will be fine," Violet said. "She's blaming the whole thing on her diet."

"Helena said, "I think underneath she really cared about Giorgio."

"Of course she did. Every woman cares about the men who make love to her, even if they're disrupters." Violet wished she weren't compelled to keep talking about her own love problems, but while she was doing it she felt as if time were standing still, death weren't even in the picture and nothing mattered that didn't concern her directly. "Roger disrupted the whole weekend for me," she said. "Sometimes I think about all the great parties he could take me to, and all the traveling, and the clothes I could buy, and I think I ought to hold on to him. The thing is, he'd need a complete makeover before he'd be marriage material. But if I drop Roger and marry Philip I'm going to be middle-class for the rest of my life."

"Hang on. Maybe he'll win a Nobel Prize," Helena said. "I just don't know how you can respect him after you've deceived him so badly."

Violet lit another cigarette and inhaled tenderly. "I feel so grateful to Philip for giving me the freedom to have him and Roger, too, it makes me love him all the more," she said.

"What about passion?"

"Passion is no problem. I want Roger when I'm with Roger. I want Philip when I'm with Philip. I think I could be passionate about anybody under the right circumstances."

"Maybe passion is what's missing in my life," Helena said. "I mean, I'm passionate about good design, I'm passionate about doing the right thing. I wanted to marry John with a passion, but I've never been passionately in love."

"Weren't you dying to know what sex was like before you had it?" Violet said. "I know you don't care about it too much now."

"To tell you the truth, I never liked penises from the first time I saw one. It was under the steering wheel in the front seat of a Thunderbird."

"I saw my brother Eddie's," Violet said.

"I still think they look like wizened old men."

"Not all the time."

"Or billy clubs," Helena said. "I was a virgin until I married Charles, you know. My mother loved him. He was very upstanding and a little repressed. You used to see us at parties—remember how he glared at people? It's not easy to be a lawyer. You have to spend your whole day arguing. He depended on me to bring pleasure into his life, but he didn't really like having pleasure. I won't tell you about the things he wanted me to do and say. I had enough trouble getting used to plain, straight sex.

"John was my next man. A German Jewish intellectual publisher who went to Hollywood High School. Someone exotic and special. As soon as I met him I knew he was for me."

"Jews aren't exotic." Violet opened her mouth wide as she inhaled, to let the cool air in. "My father's whole family are Jewish."

"John and I are very comfortable together," Helena said. "I don't know how you put passion into that."

"I think you used up all your passion trying to please your mother," Violet said. She stopped. Her other phone line had flashed at least six times. Where was Marsha, the perfect secretary? "Hold on a minute," she said, and she put Helena on hold and picked up the flashing line. It was Marsha's boyfriend, Vinnie. He always called at this hour, probably to tell Marsha what he intended to do to her later on. After the phone call Marsha always got dreamy and slow. Violet told Vinnie he could wait, put him on hold and switched back to Helena. "Hi," she said.

Helena said, "Last night my mother told me she's not afraid of death anymore, so she's not doing anything to ward it off and she thinks she may die soon. She wants to spend her last days with me."

Violet felt suddenly tired, and the afternoon was just beginning. "I thought she wanted you to have a baby before she died," she said.

"Now she wants me to write my etiquette book. She likes the title, 'The Things My Mother Taught Me.' "

"What are you going to do?" Violet said.

Helena said, "I've been thinking. When my father left us he said it was because my mother was too bossy. But I don't care about her bossiness anymore, now that I don't feel I have to obey her."

"You don't?"

"Not since I admitted to myself that I hate her sometimes. I was scared of her when I thought she was dying, though."

"I wonder if Rita hates me sometimes." Violet heard herself turning the conversation in her own direction again. Too late. Helena could interrupt if she had to.

Helena said, "I think Rita's very grown-up in some ways. When she hates you, she knows it."

"Is that supposed to make me feel good?" A vision of Rita in her tight little red bathrobe, strolling through the breakfast room at Salt Lick, assaulted Violet's equilibrium. "Helena," she said, remembering suddenly, "I haven't thanked you for letting me bring Rita this weekend. She had a wonderful time. Would you believe it? I've been so happy to have her back at school and off my mind, I forgot all about her."

"It was interesting having someone that age around," Helena said, "even if she weren't very sociable."

"Was it the pout, or the long silences? Or was it the way she wouldn't help out with the breakfast dishes?"

"Actually it was the way she wouldn't talk to anyone who wasn't a man."

"Oh, that," said Violet. "I was glad to see that. She hated men for years, you know. She had such a lousy father."

"It seemed as if she were mainly interested in them sexually," Helena said, "but maybe she's just giving the wrong impression."

Suggestions from other people that Rita might be a problem made Violet feel terribly vulnerable. Feeling vulnerable made her angry. "By the way," she said, "what got into John, talking about infidelity at the dinner table?"

Helena paused for so long that Violet didn't think she would answer at all. "Helena," she said, "are you still there?"

"I think he noticed Roger Rathbone giving me languorous looks," Helena said finally. "The fact is, the languorous looks from Roger only reminded me how glad I am to have John."

Violet hung up smiling to herself about the foolishness of vanity in women. It must have been perfectly obvious to everyone but Helena, that weekend, that Roger Rathbone's languorous looks were directed at Violet alone. In case there were any doubt, he'd just said so again on the phone this morning.

TEN

Alexandra phoned Helena on a warm Sunday afternoon six weeks later. Helena's voice was ragged at the edges, as if its trip through her windpipe had been precarious. "Did I wake you up?" Alexandra said.

"I must have been napping," Helena said. "Otherwise I couldn't have been dreaming. I dreamed I was in my nursery with my mother, only I was the mother and she was the baby, nursing at my breast."

"You have a fabulous unconscious," Alexandra said.

"Do you think so? I'm very warm. My nanny always said warm rooms give you dreams."

Alexandra said, "Did you hear my monologue on being a guest?"

"You still haven't sent me the one on eating." Helena yawned.

Alexandra felt resigned. It must be her karma to have friends who never turned on the radio. "Your weekend inspired me," she said. "I realized being a guest is like being a baby. Suddenly it's as if you don't have a life of your own to worry about. You're part of someone else's plan. You're in the arms of your host and hostess, who feed you and give you something soft to lie down on, and make sure you have a good time. So being a hostess is like being a mother."

"I think it's a mistake for a guest to think of herself as a baby." Helena had a peevish edge to her voice.

"Darling, is something the matter?" Alexandra said. "I have such good news for you, I want you to be in a good mood when you hear it."

"I am in a good mood."

"You sure, darling?"

"I'm sure."

Alexandra looked at the peaceful expression on the ivory Buddha on top of her desk. "Giorgio and I are getting married," she said. Helena didn't say anything for a full minute. The Buddha's heavy-lidded eyes reminded Alexandra of Giorgio's. "Helena, did you hear me?" she said.

"I was just trying to figure out how long you've been seeing each other."

"Six weeks, and I feel like I'm getting to know myself for the first time." Alexandra's right hand tenderly stroked her left upper arm. Mentally she prepared herself for a grilling. "I've gained three pounds since we came together. I don't care," she said. "I love him so much I could eat him up."

"Are you going to keep your maiden name?"

"What a funny question to ask first. Of course, darling, for my career. Giorgio thinks it's great I'm a public personality. He understands I wouldn't be happy if I couldn't reach out to people. After all, he phoned me up because he heard my food monologue."

"When are you going to do it?"

"The fourteenth of July. His mother will come to New York a week before. Mama Angela." Alexandra made the initial *"A"* into an "aah" sound, pronouncing her future mother-in-law's name in the Italian manner.

"How do you get along?"

"I love her. She's such a fierce mother and I have no parents at all. We talked on the phone a few days ago. She sobbed through the conversation. She kept saying, *'Mio bambino, mio bambino.'* I told her I'd take care of her baby." As if that awful conversation were happening again, Alexandra heard the static on the phone line, and Angela Scarparello's voice fading out when she started to talk about wedding plans. "I'm not good on transatlantic calls," she said. "I think it's going to be too expensive to say everything I want, so I don't even want to begin." She was going to do a focusing exercise as soon as she hung up. Once she discovered what irritated her so much about Mama Angela's voice it would stop ringing in her head.

"The way to deal with a mother-in-law," Helena said, "is to treat her like a guest. Give her total courtesy and make sure she remembers it's your place she's visiting."

Alexandra said, "I've never had a place. Not where I was really at home. I used to think I could only live with a soulmate. But Henry was a soulmate and I didn't live with him. I couldn't be in the same room with him without being physically uncomfortable."

"No one can."

"Anne-Marie can. My housekeeper. She says, 'Mr.

Henry, he have the spirit of the wanderer in him. Catch him on the fly,' and she rolls her eyes and pinches his cheeks. He loves it. Of course, Giorgio won't want Henry around our apartment when we're married."

"Aha. Is Giorgio jealous?"

"He says he'd like to do Henry the favor of being jealous, but he doesn't even feel to him like a man. So I guess the answer is yes, he's jealous."

"I've never really had a conversation with Giorgio," Helena said. "What does he talk about?"

Alexandra refused to be intimidated by Helena's unstated disapproval. "Giorgio and I are into creature comforts. Food, flowers, furniture. We lounge around with each other. There's nothing intellectual about it," she said. "I was worn out from thinking. Being with Henry was like listening to Ravi Shankar on the sitar all day, one raga after another. It was difficult and it made me feel pure. Giorgio is more like Western classical music. When we have croissants with strawberry jam and home-ground Colombian coffee for breakfast, and there are tulips on the table, and we look into each other's eyes, it's as if there's Mozart playing in the background even though there isn't any music at all. I've always wanted a life with Mozart as the background music."

"Mozart wasn't Italian," Helena said.

"Well, whoever the Italian Mozart was. Vivaldi."

Helena said, "But you used to say Giorgio was empty."

"What I meant was I could breathe around Giorgio. I didn't understand that then. I thought I needed a man to look up to, and I would be his muse." Out her window, Alexandra watched a plane, very high in the sky, very free, like a big bat soaring past all the tallest buildings in New York. "But now I'm doing my monologues, and what I need is a man like Giorgio to inspire me, someone who listens, and doesn't answer back and criticize the way most men do. Anyway, he's not really empty, he's like a new blackboard—what you write on it is very clear because there isn't a lot of old stuff only half-erased beneath the surface."

"If you're happy I'm very happy for you," Helena said.

Alexandra felt full of love: specific love for Giorgio, and universal love for everyone else in the world. "You're the first friend I've told," she said. "I want to ask your advice, darling. I'm thinking of doing a monologue on marriage. I could announce it to all my listeners that way. I could send out news releases to the press about the monologue."

"What's wrong with a simple announcement in *The New York Times?*" Helena yawned. "Excuse me," she said. "I don't know why I should be yawning."

It was obvious Helena would rather go to sleep than express emotion, but you couldn't tell her that. "I'll probably announce it in the *Times*. I want my listeners to hear it from me, though," Alexandra said. "I have some ideas about marriage I want to share with them. I'm going to send Kitty two dozen American beauty roses and a thank-you note."

"I don't think you need to thank her," Helena said. "After all, you knew him first."

"I'd like to do something special for her." Alexandra pictured Kitty behind the delicacies counter at Luxury Foods, in the midst of pâtés, risottos and ceviches, smiling so all her white teeth gleamed, a little like a shark's teeth. "I used to be jealous of Kitty because she could eat as much as she wanted without getting fat," she said, "but now that I'm happy all my anger has disappeared. In fact I don't know what I would have done without her. It wasn't until she tried to steal Giorgio away from me that I came to my senses. I found out that I love him madly."

Helena yawned. "Excuse me for yawning again," she said. "Why don't you have Luxury Foods do the food for your wedding? Then Kitty will get something out of it, too."

"That's a great idea. I can include that in the news release," Alexandra said. "You know how Kitty loves publicity."

Alexandra hung up smiling. Now that she'd decided to become a married woman it was as if she'd crossed a great ocean, and she looked back with amazement at her old self who'd been in a single girl's limbo for so long, always a displaced person, always thinking in terms of the future, when maybe she'd meet a man who'd make her life okay.

She had a first line for her monologue already. She took a fresh yellow pad from the top desk drawer, slipped it into her new silver plastic clipboard and wrote, "Marriage, darlings, is what you do to settle down. At least that's what they tell me. I want to know if you can settle down and still have a wonderful life, so as soon as I can get the arrangements made, I'm getting married."

When Helena hung up she could barely keep her eyes open. She didn't know what could account for such extreme fatigue, beyond the effort of trying to support a friend. Naturally she was happy Alexandra was happy, but now she was going to have to find something to like about Giorgio, a man who traveled with a separate suitcase just for his shoes—running shoes, moccasins, tennis shoes, pointy-toed Italian oxfords, loafers, riding boots, for God's sake—and smiled at you as if he knew more about your body than you did. John was in his library next door with his fire hat on. Helena's eyelids felt so heavy. She asked herself what upset her about men in costumes. Did they look as if they wanted to stop being strong and manly and usurp the woman's role? Who would be head of the family in that case?

Maybe she could think this over better in the chintz guest room. She never went in there, normally. It reminded her of her mother's apartment where all the overstuffed furniture and the roses and lilacs and ruffles were designed to make you think you were safe at home. She wished she were safe at home. The clean smell of lavender overtook her when she opened the door. She lay down on the bed and fell asleep before she could remember what the question was.

A half hour later—in fact as soon as Philip left her apartment for his mother's—Violet called Helena. Helena's voice sounded husky. Violet was on her chaise longue in her new pale peach tap pants and camisole, facing her three new potted palms. "I didn't wake you up, did I?" she said. "It's the middle of the afternoon."

Helena said, "I've been sleepy all day."

Violet decided to warm up the atmosphere before she plunged in and told her news. "It's probably age," she said. "I was just looking at myself in the mirror. I'm getting sag flaps."

"Sag flaps?"

"You know, those creases that run from your nose to your mouth? They make me look like a hag."

"They don't make you look like a hag," said Helena tartly. "I've had them since I was a little girl."

"But I haven't." It was just like secretive Helena to expect you to know she was sensitive about her sag flaps, even though she never acknowledged she had them. You put up with your old friends' faults because when you called them you felt as if there were someone there on the receiving end. "How's John?" Violet said, in order to repair the gaffe and show her interest in Helena's life.

"In his library looking at a new old book. I'm in the chintz guest room. It's cozy here."

"I wonder if Philip will develop hobbies and collections once we're living together. Right now he says he's fascinated with me."

"I think I'm lucky John has his books, and his flute. Otherwise I'd never have time for my friends," Helena said.

"When I was married to Stanley he was always telling me I talked too much. I've been afraid to live with a man ever since. I'm afraid I don't know how." Violet adjusted the camisole strap on her left shoulder. She hadn't any idea why she'd just said that, when in fact she'd recently decided to try again after all.

Helena was silent for twenty seconds at least. Then she said, "You probably shouldn't live with a man again. You have more freedom to do what you want this way."

"But I want to live with Philip."

Helena interrupted. "Alexandra and Giorgio are getting married," she said. "I don't think that's a good idea, either."

"I don't believe you." Violet's love of gossip began a struggle inside with her desire to focus her attention on herself.

"Before Kitty got her hands on him she used to say he was a pest. Now she says he's great to lounge around with. I don't think he's changed at all," Helena said. "I suppose it's a positive sign she's interested in lounging around."

"Giorgio's very rich, you know." Violet had a moment of fury with Philip for not being very rich. She let it pass. "Alexandra won't ever have to work again."

"She wants to work, she says."

That was enough about Alexandra. Violet's heart was beating as if something had frightened her. "Philip just asked me to marry him and I said yes," she said as fast as she could.

"Helena said, "That's great. It's about time."

Violet said, "Don't you want to know when? The fourteenth of July."

The silence made Violet feel as if a judgment were being passed. After a little while Helena said, "You'd better talk to Alexandra. I'm pretty sure she's getting married on the fourteenth of July."

"She can't." Violet got a stick of licorice root from a small tin box on her bedside table and began to gnaw on it. The bark tasted like tobacco but it didn't satisfy her nicotine craving. "That's when my mother and stepfather will be in town." She stopped. "What did you mean when you said, 'It's about time'?" she said. "Do you think I'm making a mistake?"

"Not if you're sure."

"I'm pretty sure."

"Where are you going to live?"

"At my apartment."

"You're making a mistake," Helena said. "You should get a new apartment together."

"I like my apartment."

"How can you live with Philip in a place you lived in with Stanley?"

"It makes me feel good about myself to know Stanley had to give it to me. He told me it was one of the best investments he ever made."

"Is Philip keeping his apartment?"

"I think he should sublet it. He says, where will he go if I kick him out."

"If you get a new apartment together, neither of you will be in a position to kick the other out," Helena said. "At your place you've already made the rules. It's not fair to him."

"I need all the advantages I can get. I'll be devastated if this doesn't work out." Violet's left eyelid twitched. She bit off a piece of licorice bark and mashed it between her front teeth.

"Take my advice and make up new rules with him right away. And get some new furniture together," Helena said.

"I don't like Philip's taste. He's a scientist. I know he's brilliant when it comes to taking minuscule pieces of frog chromosomes and attaching them to human chromosomes, but his apartment is a Gothic horror. His mother's apartment is a Gothic horror, too. She gave him his furniture. Her mother brought it over from Germany. It's all heavy, dark chests, and velvet sofas with antimacassars on them."

"At least make sure he brings a few pieces with him. Otherwise he won't feel at home. You can cover them gradually with quilts and afghans, and move them back out."

Other people's solutions always sounded more complicated than the problems they were meant to solve. Just hearing them made Violet feel helpless. "What am I going to do about Philip's compulsive neatness?" she said. She wished she knew how to keep quiet and solve things for herself. "When I leave clothes lying around he folds them and puts them away for me. Then I can never find them again, and I get angry. If he picks up after me I'll be angry all the time."

"Make it one of the rules that each one picks up after himself. You'll probably need a time limit, too, for how long you can leave a mess lying around. Then if he touches your things, you'll have some leverage when he gets mad at you for bad behavior."

Violet said, "If you don't think I'm making a mistake, why are you giving me a lecture?"

"I think you ought to know what you're doing," Helena said. "Being married isn't very romantic, you know. You have to work at it. Without letting your husband know you're working at it, if you want to keep him happy."

Violet regarded her leafy palms, which reminded her of Roger. Incorporating the spirit of Roger into her bedroom, in the form of palms, would make bedtime more exotic and help her remain faithful to Philip. "I think working at love is very romantic," she said.

Helena said, "John likes to do our food shopping. Most of the time I let him. If your husband wants to do something for you, you ought to let him. The trouble is, he's not as good at choosing fruits and vegetables as I am. But I put up with his fruits and vegetables. Actually, I don't always like the cuts of meat he buys, either. I eat them. If I didn't he'd be hurt. Not only that, I'd have to do the shopping myself. Don't think it's easy, having to consider somebody else's feelings all the time."

"I love the idea of someone else considering my feelings all the time," Violet said.

"If you take advantage of someone else's good nature, sooner or later God will punish you. Even the Indians believe that," Helena said.

"Doesn't John always give you what you want?"

"He knows I'm nicer to be around when I like the way things are going."

Violet had a moment of admiration for John for bearing

with Helena day after day, Rebecca or not. "Well, Philip gives me everything I want, too, now that I tell him what I want," she said. "And I give him what he wants. I tell him when he hurts my feelings. He tells me when I hurt his feelings. I really like men who don't get hurt feelings, but I understand Philip is more modern than I am. We never argue. I have Roger to fight with. That's the problem. I'm afraid I'm going to be awful to Philip the way I was before, when I get married and give Roger up."

"You could just stop being awful," Helena said. "Make up your mind not to argue. You're not going to win points for proving you're right, you know. Think of how much prettier you look when you're smiling."

"But if I'm good to Philip, and I have no one else in my life, there won't be anything mysterious about me. He'll find out I'm boring and he'll leave."

"I think Philip is the kind of man who needs a woman to take care of. As long as you appreciate him, he'll never leave you."

"Do you really think so?" Violet said. "Maybe that's why we're so good together."

There was the click of another call coming in on Helena's line. "Hold on a minute, okay?" she said.

Violet got up and found an old shopping list in the drawer in her bedside table. She wrote on the back of it, "Rules." This conversation was exhilarating to her, in the same way learning a new game was exhilarating, or anticipating the arrival of a new appliance like a food processor that would change your life. She wrote down, "Each one picks up after himself" and "Time limit." She wondered if she could live by rules.

Helena came back on the line. "Sorry," she said.

Violet said, "Maybe I'll let Philip have Rita's room as a

workroom and she can take it back when she's home. Do you think that would be violating her space?"

"Uh huh," Helena said.

"But I don't want to give him the dining room. If I do we can't give dinner parties, and no one will invite us anywhere."

"Be careful," Helena said. "Philip's going to be Rita's stepfather."

"I don't think Rita wants a stepfather." An image from the weekend came into Violet's mind. Philip, standing near the living room window, telling Rita a joke; Rita, lolling in a chair, looking him up and down as if he were flirting with her. Rita was just beginning to be beautiful in a sullen-mouthed way. Violet knew it was normal for mothers to be jealous of their daughters' youth; she was afraid to describe this upsetting scene to anyone. "Right now Rita treats Philip like someone on her level only not as hip," she said. "He likes soft rock and he wears his hair too long."

"You'd better make it clear she has to obey him."

"The trouble is, he wants her to accept him so badly he'll even take her side against me."

"Maybe you ought to go to a marriage counselor."

"Very funny." Violet rubbed her right hand on her satiny tummy. At least her underwear felt great, even if, no matter what she did, her life never seemed to work right.

"Lots of people do it before they get married," Helena said. "That was Kitty on the other line. I have to call her back. She's got the new issue of *Gossip* with her story in it."

"How does she sound?"

"They gave her four pages. She says each one is worth at least a hundred thousand dollars to her."

"Good luck," Violet said.

"Congratulations to you. I mean it," said Helena.

"Isn't it rude to say 'Congratulations' to the bride? It sounds as if she were lucky to find someone to marry her. I thought you only said it to the groom."

"That used to be true. Modern etiquette is more realistic," Helena said. "Anyway, I mean congratulations for making up your mind."

Helena hadn't thought about Kitty's party since the morning after, when the only thing she could remember about her conversation with Judy Thaxter was that she'd had it. Now, as if it were yesterday, she saw herself sitting on the window seat between Judy and Larry Atwill. She recalled the pleasure of having someone take notes while she talked. She remembered Judy's soothing voice. Judy said, "I hear Kitty's mother is in a mental hospital and her father's an alcoholic. Is that true?"

Helena saw her own back straighten. "Not at all," she heard herself say indignantly. "They're ordinary farmers in Longpond, Ohio." She didn't know why this scene had vanished from consciousness only to appear to her now, just in time to make a defense of ignorance difficult should she have any reason to defend herself.

"Are you upset?" Helena said as soon as Kitty answered.

"How could I be upset? I'm four hundred thousand dollars ahead."

Helena held her breath. Kitty might be waiting for her to put her foot in it. "What did they say about you?" she said after forty-five seconds in which no words came to her.

"They open with a photograph of Aphrodisia and me on a hill in Central Park. It looks like the moors—except for the skyline. I'm standing in profile. She's straining at the leash, looking up as if she's spotted a wild duck in the sky.

The headline is 'Hunting for Taste Sensations.' Whippets hunt rabbits, but so what?"

"Then you like it?"

"They say I'm a good businesswoman. There's some interesting stuff about how I choose the products I sell in the store. They even put in my taste test."

"What's your taste test?"

"My taste test. First I sniff the food, for aroma. Then I roll it around my tongue so it hits all my taste buds. I push it against the roof of my mouth for texture, and I bite it for sound effects. I make terrible faces. The salesperson is watching me all this time and getting nervous. If the food has any peculiarities I find out about them. I only decide to stock a new food if I get a chill while I'm tasting it. That's what I call the shiver that goes up my spine when I'm having pleasure."

"The shiver would go *down* your spine if it was coming from your taste buds," Helena said.

"They made a crack I didn't like," Kitty said. "Here it is:

'Curtiss, a willowy blonde who would look good arching a bow, also hunts for the sport of it. Those who want to be catty about Kitty say her private life is a hunt for sensations of other kinds.'

"That's innuendo, isn't it? Judy Thaxter says she didn't do it. She says the editors put everything into *Gossip* style. If they mean I like sex and drugs, what's so catty about saying that?"

With her right foot Helena pulled over the chintz ottoman that matched the chair she was sitting on. She put both feet up. Provisionally, she was beginning to experience relief. "That's *Gossip* style," she said. "John won't publish *Gossip* writers. They can't resist saying 'catty about Kitty.' It could be a lot worse."

"I know," Kitty said. "The first time I read this I almost died. I felt as if I were pinned against the wall and someone was throwing knives at me. Now I realize, even though the story's about me, it's really nothing personal. It's a chance for the magazine to say something about food preferences. I'm just the object."

"They didn't even say right out you like sex and drugs."

"I could sue them if they did. I could sue Judy Thaxter for interviewing my parents."

"Your parents?" Helena shoved the ottoman away and sat up straight. Her throat constricted so she had to push her voice through it. "I thought they were dead," she said.

Kitty said, "I told you my parents were still on the farm in Longpond, Ohio."

"You did? I don't remember."

"I don't know who could have told Judy about them, but I'd love to find out."

"Whoever it was, I bet you want to kill her," Helena said.

"Not really. They got good quotes. My mother said she wasn't surprised I was successful in the food business since I was always a picky eater. I think that's very witty. My father said I was his favorite daughter. When I read that I started to cry. I don't know why he never told me."

"You see, your parents love you after all. I'm very relieved for your sake." Helena considered confessing her indiscretion. If she hadn't forgotten, she told herself, she'd have done the right thing and made the confession long ago when Kitty could have done something about it. Was there any point, now that it was too late? No point except setting the record straight. Of course, that would give Kitty the right to get angry. Helena would rather listen to a fingernail scraping on a blackboard than to the sounds of an anger she'd inspired. She let practicality prevail. Why complicate a matter that was already settled between friends? "Your father probably thought when you were younger it would have gone to your head," she said. "My mother told me she loved me for the first time in her life last week. It's something she learned at Heart Throb House. They told her expressing her feelings would help prevent another heart attack. She said, 'I told them it was terrible manners, but if it was good for my health I'd try it.'"

"Why is expressing your feelings such terrible manners?"

"It might make someone else who doesn't have any feelings uncomfortable. At least that's the way I always understood it."

Kitty said, "My old roommate Alison called. The one who had the affair with the senator's wife? She saw my story in an advance copy of *Gossip*. She wants to have dinner with me."

"You'll probably get hundreds of calls like that after a story in *Gossip*," Helena said.

"I haven't heard from Henry all week."

"Never mind Henry." Helena spoke as if enough enthusiasm could make up for all her sins. "Tomorrow night maybe Mister Right will read about you."

"Alison is worse than a man," Kitty said. "She wanted to know how my breasts got twice as big as they used to be."

"Is that some kind of wisecrack?" Helena was definitely queasy. She cupped her own breasts with her hands. They were full and terribly tender. "You need some nice, normal people in your life," she said.

Kitty said, "Alison is a nice, normal lesbian. Henry's a

nice, normal mental health professional. Giorgio's a nice, normal Italian millionaire who likes powder puffs better than strong women. Who's to say what's nice and normal?"

"I don't know," Helena said, "but if I don't get off this phone and lie down I'm going to be sick."

"You shouldn't let me upset you so much," Kitty said. "I only do it to tease."

"Actually, it's not you that's upsetting me." Helena held on to the reassuring chintz on the arms of her chair and cleared her throat. "Don't tell anybody," she said, "but this time I think I'm pregnant."

ELEVEN

Even a woman's plans for happiness may cost her anxious moments. For instance, Alexandra spent a full day worrying nonstop about calling Kitty. When she tried to imagine herself telling Kitty she was marrying Giorgio, she saw Kitty's face as if it were doing a yoga exercise to ward off wrinkles: first it crumpled toward its own center, like a fist clenched in rage, then it opened wide as Kitty began to scream her accusations. Alexandra didn't want to interfere with her own good feelings by having such a scene occur. It wasn't until she realized, late Monday afternoon, that she was getting depressed simply from the strain of anticipating the scene, that she dialed Kitty's number.

"Darling, I want you to be the first to know," she said, as soon as she heard Kitty's voice. "Giorgio and I are getting married."

Kitty said, "Congratulations."

Alexandra strained to hear the emotional content of Kitty's response. There didn't appear to be any. "Aren't you mad at me?" she said.

"For what?"

"I don't know. Because you can't marry him now."

"Maybe you'd like the dog," Kitty said in the same neutral voice.

"The dog?"

"Aphrodisia. For a wedding present. She and Giorgio are very close."

"Thanks," Alexandra said. Though she liked the idea of being in intimate contact with everything Giorgio loved, she wasn't sure she wanted another living being sharing their new apartment—especially one that smelled of Kitty. "Can I let you know?"

"Sure," Kitty said. "Did you see the piece about me in *Gossip?*"

"No, darling. When?"

"This week. Tell Giorgio they had it all set up to open with a big picture of me with him and Aphro. There was a paragraph devoted to his ideas about racing-car design. Of course they had to redo the whole thing after I broke up with him."

Poor Kitty. Alexandra had no intention of telling Giorgio any such thing. "I hope we can hire Luxury Foods to cook for our wedding reception, darling. It will make all the difference." She said this with so much sincerity she brought tears to her own eyes. "We're getting married the fourteenth of July. I'll invite the major columnists."

"Someone called this morning about franchising Luxury Foods, Ltd., all over Texas," Kitty said. "Do you have listeners in Texas?"

"Are you kidding? They listen to me all over the country."

"Talk to your demographics department, okay? I've got to run, hon. Five calls waiting." Kitty hung up.

Alexandra had accomplished what she'd set out to do, and yet she felt unsatisfied. Her head was full of the blandishments she hadn't had to use to conquer Kitty's resistance. She thought about the refrigerator where the chocolate-chocolate-chip ice cream was, waiting to be this evening's dessert. If this were six weeks ago, without a doubt she would have been in the kitchen gorging herself already. The reason she was so happy now was, she could telephone Giorgio and sweet-talk him, instead.

It took Violet three days before she could bear the idea that she wasn't the only person of her acquaintance getting married this July. She finally called Alexandra at lunchtime on Thursday while she was waiting for her baby shrimp salad on rye to be delivered. Baby shrimps, with tender green chunks of celery in creamy mayonnaise, reminded her of flowered sheets and wedding bouquets for the bride who's been married before. "I hear you and Giorgio are getting married in July," she said.

"Oh, darling, I wanted to tell you myself."

"Helena told me when I told her Philip and I are getting married in July."

"You are? How fabulous. When did you decide?"

"Decide? We've been working up to it for three years," Violet said. "I hear you want to do it the fourteenth of July."

"That's right. You'll get an invitation, darling. I've just begun to make plans. It's such an enormous change for me. I feel a little weird this week. Not sick, exactly, but probably the way a snake feels when it sheds its skin—a little shaky and sorrowful about what's going out of my life, even though it's useless and means nothing to me anymore."

"What's going out of your life?"

"I mean the old me. The one who didn't want to grow up and take responsibilities and live with anyone."

"I don't think you should rush into it," Violet said. "Why not take the time to get used to your new state?"

"But I won't be in my new state until I'm married," Alexandra said. "Right now it's as if I'm sitting in a waiting room, and that's what brings the sadness up."

"I don't feel as if I'm in a waiting room. I'm ready to buy my dress and order flowers. We figured it out. The fourteenth of July is the only time we can do it."

"The fourteenth of July? Oh, no, darling. You have to find another date."

"My mother and stepfather will be in town. Besides, Philip and I have been in love much longer than you and Giorgio. We should have first priority."

"Giorgio and I were lovers from another life," Alexandra said in a throaty voice. "I kept away from him in this lifetime. I knew once I opened up to him it would be very serious."

"So now you think the sooner you get married the sooner all your worries will be over." Violet felt as if she were talking to a child. "Of course you're excited about getting married, but believe me, I've been there. You're just the same after you're married as you were before. If sadness comes up for you, sadness will still come up for you."

"I like the fourteenth of July. It's the French Independence Day. My mother's mother was French."

Violet would have to get an intermediary to speak to Alexandra. You couldn't argue with someone who didn't operate on the same practical level you did. "Listen," she said. "I've just sprung this on you. Why don't you think about it?"

"I think about it all the time, darling," Alexandra said. "I've already asked Kitty to do the food."

"What did she say when you told her you were marrying Giorgio?"

"She didn't say. She seemed more interested in her article in *Gossip*. Did you see it?"

"I thought they made her sound too ambitious."

"My darling, she is too ambitious," said Alexandra. "The man she was in love with six weeks ago is marrying one of her best friends and she isn't even upset. I had tears in my eyes, on the phone with her. All she could talk about was some people who want to franchise her business in Texas."

"She's going to make a fortune on that article. I hope she remembers her friends who buttered up the reporter for her." Marsha entered Violet's office with a brown paper bag, which she placed on her desk. Violet grabbed the sandwich out. Baby shrimp salad. If she were Kitty she could be having caviar for lunch. "You know," she said, pushing her food aside so she wouldn't be tempted to chew in Alexandra's ear, "in my mind marriage has always meant financial security. The truth is, Philip doesn't make much more money than I do. I've been thinking about keeping my maiden name. Well, actually it's my first married name. I'd do it if I didn't absolutely love being Mrs. Someone."

"I like the women whose announcements in the paper say 'The bride will keep her name.' It makes them seem feminine and also serious," Alexandra said. "I don't want to turn into someone else when I get married."

Violet hadn't meant to get into a conversation about knowing who you are. In her opinion, if you were over thirty and didn't know who you were, you shouldn't go around talking about it. "Are you going to wear white?" she said.

"Off-white."

"Now that you don't have to be a virgin to wear white, I don't see the point," Violet said.

"It's just traditional for brides. The same way Santa Claus wears red and has a white beard."

"A woman who's never been married might have had three thousand lovers. It's okay for her to wear white," Violet said. "But if you've been married just once, even if you've only slept with one man, white doesn't look right."

"Only slept with one man, darling? Who are you talking about?"

Just Violet's luck, the middle of lunchtime and her intercom was buzzing. "Excuse me a minute," she said to Alexandra. She picked up the other line and heard the fretful voice of Glenda Crane. Glenda was on a surprise visit to New York before shooting began on her new picture, and she wanted to know why no one had met her at the airport. Violet made a lunch date with Glenda. This afternoon she'd find a gossip columnist to come along and get the exclusive interview. She wrote Frannie Stuyvesant's name at the top of her list of things to do. At the subway party, Frannie had monopolized "Big Risk" and "Cherry Bomb"—who were two very sexy black adolescents—and then she hadn't printed a word about them, so as far as Violet was concerned Frannie owed her a favor. Violet switched back to Alexandra. There was more she had to say about white wedding dresses. "I bought a bride's magazine with an article about remarriage," she said. "It said you could wear white if that was what you really wanted. That sounded as if nobody you'd take seriously would even want to wear white at her second wedding. I don't know why not. I loved being a bride. Marching down the aisle in a white dress with a train makes a woman feel special. It was better than being a wife, really."

"Don't you think big, traditional weddings are a little bit girlish for women our age?" Alexandra said. "Giorgio and I are going to have a small, dignified ceremony in a nice, quiet Catholic church. I hope they let you take 'obey' out of the ceremony in a Catholic church. Then we'll have a big reception for all our friends, and we'll move into our new apartment together. We've seen one we want to buy on East Fifty-seventh Street."

"We're going to live at my place," Violet said.

"Oh, really. That should be nice and cozy, darling."

Violet said, "We're not planning to have any more children." In fact, in the daydream she'd been having when Freddy got mad at her at the office, she was bending over a crib with a naked, screaming baby boy in it. The baby kicked his little legs and wagged his little prick in the air. To make the screaming stop, Violet knew all she had to do was pick him up and hug him. The daydream made her feel equal in power to Freddy.

"I'm going to Smith's tomorrow to pick out our china and silver and put them on the bridal gifts registry," Alexandra said.

"The bridal gifts registry," Violet said. "Lucky you, the blushing bride. Philip and I will probably get married in a judge's chambers. I can wear a pale linen suit. Rita will be with us, and Philip's mother, my mother and stepfather, my brother Eddie, and a few of my closest friends if they can make it. I suppose they'll all want to go to your wedding instead. It will be more festive. First weddings are supposed to be festive. Second weddings are supposed to be subdued." Violet stopped. The possibility of having to endure the fate she'd just described was giving her stomach cramps. She ran her right index finger around the rim of her sandwich and daintily put the finger into her mouth.

Alexandra said, "Listen, darling, maybe we can work something out."

"How can we? We have all the same friends. We'll probably both want Kitty to do the food. Probably you've already hired Gordon's friend Alistair to be the photographer."

"What a wonderful idea," Alexandra said.

Violet said, "I left a message on his machine yesterday."

"Maybe one of us could get married in the morning and the other in the evening."

"The guests wouldn't be very fresh for the second wedding." Violet eyed her sandwich. She reminded herself how insignificant she felt, compared to the food they were involved with, when anyone chewed in her ear. She took a stale pack of cigarettes from her right-hand top drawer and lit one.

"What are you going to do about music?" Alexandra said. "I thought we'd hire Paul Arnold and his band. He calls himself Paulo now. They play New Wave Afro Brazilian jazz."

"You mean Paulo and the Flappers, right?"

"The Flippers, darling, Paulo and the Flippers. They're going to have a big hit with their new song, 'The Lobster Samba.' The lyrics are great. If only I could remember them. The idea is, when lobsters move around in the ocean they do a wonderful dance, but humans only love lobsters once they turn red. And when they turn red they can't dance anymore. It's a lesson about letting things be what they are."

"I guess you have to hear it," Violet said.

"You know what?" said Alexandra. "I just had an idea. You want to get married the fourteenth of July. I want to get married the fourteenth of July. We're good friends, right? Why don't we have a double wedding?"

"I don't know," Violet said. "Do Philip and Giorgio like each other?"

"I don't think they pay much attention to each other."

"Philip's an atheist. He won't want to get married by a priest."

"We could have the ceremonies separately. I could invite the press to the church. Then we'd have a private double reception afterwards."

"It's okay if you want to invite the press to the reception." Violet imagined a write-up in *The New York Times*. She'd say something memorable. They'd run a big picture. With the right kind of media attention she could easily become a star.

"Helena wouldn't like that," Alexandra said. "Couldn't you picture the reception at Helena's apartment?"

"You're right. I'll call her," Violet said. She stubbed out her cigarette, which she'd smoked down to the filter. "I'll tell her she'll be saving the life of her oldest friend. She won't be able to refuse me. Now if only I could stop smoking everything would be perfect."

"But you stopped two years ago, didn't you?"

"I started again after the weekend at Helena's," Violet said. "I don't know if I'm doing the right thing, committing myself to Philip, and no one can tell me. When there's something in my mouth I don't have to think about it."

"I guess I'm addicted to Giorgio now," said Alexandra.

"For one thing, my skin is a lot better than it was when I was addicted to food."

Before Violet called Helena she asked Marsha to intercept all her calls, took off her shoes and tucked her feet under her in her swivel chair. "What's up?" she said when Helena answered. She tried to pretend it was Saturday late morning and she was snuggled under the covers, talking girl to girl, but the metal desk she was sitting behind, and the file cabinets she faced, had nothing of the pampered woman's bedroom about them.

"I guess I was napping," Helena said. She spoke as if her voice were submerged in heavy syrup.

"It's not good for you to sleep so much during the day, is it? How can you fall asleep at night?"

"It's a new phase with me. The more I sleep the more I want to sleep. I don't think it can be bad, or I wouldn't enjoy it so much."

"I've been sleeping too much lately, but I'm not enjoying it." Violet swiveled her chair around so she faced the poster Stan had given her, of Rita Hayworth in *Gilda*. The sight of Rita standing there in her strapless dress, smoking, laughing, trailing her fur, made Violet wish she'd been born just a little bit earlier, in a simpler time, when to be a glamour girl was enough. Stan used to say she looked like a young Rita Hayworth but she didn't, really. Her features were thinner, and she could never master that raised eyebrow and expectant smile. Now that she was getting married again, it was probably time she got rid of the long hair, too.

"I think people sleep a lot when there are things they don't want to face," she said. "I know I start yawning every time I think about Alexandra having her wedding the same day as mine. Last night Philip and I went to that new twenties musical and I nodded off in the middle of the bubble fan dance. While I was trying to make sense of the plot, I was trying to figure out which of our friends would go to her wedding and which to mine if they all got both invitations in the same mail delivery."

"That will never happen," Helena said.

"I only brought it up because we were talking about brain fatigue."

Helena said, "I'm sleeping a lot because now I'm sleeping for two. Soon I'm going to start knitting little things."

"Sleeping for two?" Violet stopped swiveling and faced front. "Do you mean you're pregnant? How far gone are you?"

"A month and a half. Don't tell anybody, okay?"

"That's great. But I thought you decided you didn't want a baby."

"Maybe you thought that because I stopped talking about it. What I decided was to try to go along with whatever happened. If I was too uptight to get pregnant, that would probably mean I wasn't meant to be a mother. If John was beginning to sound like a movie Nazi to me, I could still be open to him the way he is. I must have relaxed for a few minutes, just at the right time. It probably happened that weekend at Salt Lick. Now all I think about is the cells dividing and subdividing inside of me, getting ready to be arms and legs and sex organs. I feel like, the more there is of *it,* the less there is of me to keep it under control. What if I move too suddenly and dislodge it?"

"You know the fetus doesn't go to sleep when you do," Violet said.

Helena said, "I wish I were the fetus. I thought pregnancy was supposed to make you radiant. I'm so scared I can hardly breathe. How am I going to know how to behave toward this child? What if it and I don't like each other? That could easily happen. What if it's ugly? I hope it's a boy; then its looks won't matter so much."

"I bet John is happy," Violet said.

"He's treating me like a Jewish mother already. He gives me pillows wherever I sit. My mother says she's too young to be a grandmother. She's sixty-eight."

"You'll see," Violet said. "The baby will give her something to live for."

"She told me she was sick the whole time she was pregnant with me."

"You're just having the pregnancy blues." Violet lit a cigarette.

"I've never heard of pregnancy blues."

"It's lucky you're having them so early," Violet said. "By the fourteenth of July you'll be feeling great. You won't really be showing yet, but you'll be blooming. Your breasts will be big and juicy."

Helena said, "Please don't mention juicy breasts. Someone told me a terrible story the other night about a mother who was weaning her baby. She was at her first dinner party in months, having a wonderful time. Then, in the middle of the story she was telling to the man on her left, she heard a Siamese cat howl, and her breasts came on like fountains. She squirted the poor man's jacket right through her lace blouse."

Violet said, "This will be long before you're nursing. I'd like you to be my matron of honor."

"You're not going to have a big, formal wedding, are you? It's your second marriage."

"I'd just like you to be with me that day," Violet said.

"I'd love to," said Helena. "Does that mean I'll have to miss Alexandra's wedding?"

"I was just talking to her. Not only do we have the same friends, but we both want Kitty to do the food, and we want the same photographer and the same band to play."

"What band?"

"Paulo and the Flippers. They have that new record, 'The Lobster Samba.' "

"Oh, yes, that's a good song," Helena said, and she sang, "When the lobsters samba, the lobsters samba/All the water in the ocean sways."

"The only answer is probably a double reception. But where will we ever find a place that feels right to all of us that we can possibly afford?"

Helena was silent.

Violet said, "Helena?"

"I'm counting," Helena said. "We could have it here, but I'm not sure how busy John's going to be. In July he'll be breaking in a new secretary."

Violet put her cigarette in an ashtray and her feet on the floor. "New secretary," she said. "You're full of surprises today."

"Rebecca's moving to Los Angeles. She's got a job with a big-time movie producer. Al something. I can't remember his name. She told John it was an offer she couldn't refuse. I don't know where he'll find anybody as devoted to her job. She certainly simplified my life."

It made Violet angry the way some people seemed to get everything they wanted in life, just by keeping themselves ignorant of their own true circumstances. That was why she'd had trouble worrying about Helena all along. "I'd love to have the reception at your place," she said, "if John doesn't mind."

"Maybe I'll announce the baby at the party. We'll know its sex by then," Helena said.

"Sure. You could do that." Violet bit the cuticle of her wedding ring finger. She was glad it was her second marriage and she was a mature woman with a teen-aged daughter. A younger, more foolish woman would have made a fuss when she found out that for things to be right she'd have to share the spotlight on her wedding day with two of her closest friends.

"I'm sure it will be a boy," Helena said. "A boy is what I want. I'll wear white with blue flowers."

"It will be a terrific party," said Violet, who wanted to get off the phone before she said anything about who should wear white and who shouldn't that might spoil Helena's enthusiasm.

"You caught me on the way into the bath," Kitty said when Violet finally got a chance to call her that evening. "I'm wearing my new leopard terry cloth sarong."

"I have some good gossip for you," Violet said. "Rebecca is moving to California. Maybe that's why she got rid of her cat."

"Moving to California. Do you think she's pregnant?" Kitty said.

"No, it's Helena who's pregnant."

"That's a secret," Kitty said.

"I guess she's told John."

"Yes, but you shouldn't be telling me."

"You already know," Violet said, "so don't be petty."

Kitty said, "So John is giving up Rebecca for Helena's sake, now that Helena's having his child."

"It's too bad Helena doesn't appreciate his gesture. She's afraid the next one won't be as devoted to her job as Rebecca was." The way Violet saw it, to live with her husband through two years of his affair with his secretary, from its blossoming to its death, and never suspect a thing, a woman had to have a particular kind of insulation sheathing her nerves. Thinking about Helena's insulation made Violet feel chilly. She stared out her living room window at a brave little tugboat going by in the river. She wished Philip were with her.

"Henry says Helena needs to learn to love herself," Kitty said.

Violet said, "Henry. I don't know how you can trust a man who doesn't like sex."

"I think sex is something different for him than it is for us."

"Come on. You mean he likes it the way frogs do it? She lays the eggs and then he swims over them and sprays them with fertilizer? He's human, isn't he?"

"If I tell you something, will you promise not to tell?" Kitty said.

"Of course." Violet prepared herself to pay attention to what was coming next.

Kitty said, "I'm having the best sex with Henry I've ever had in my life. He does it by chanting."

"Boy, did Alexandra get her signals crossed. You mean he chants and fucks at the same time?"

"This may sound bizarre to you. He doesn't do any physical fucking at all," Kitty said. "I experience his chanting on the physical plane. It started after I'd been on the diet a few weeks."

"I don't think it's a good idea to change yourself around inside. How do you know what you'll bring out?"

"I lie down and relax," Kitty said. "I wear loose clothes. Henry chants. He can chant for hours without getting winded. I lie as still as I can. At first he goes slow, and the sound he makes is like the softest breeze blowing over my body. Later he goes faster and faster. It's as if the words were tongues. They drive me wild. When I come I feel as if I've exploded."

"Whatever turns you on," Violet said. You expected weirdness from Alexandra, it was part of her personality, but it was inappropriate in someone who was becoming a self-made millionaire. "Does Henry explode, too?"

"He doesn't even know. He thinks I'm in spiritual ecstasy."

"If he doesn't know I don't think you can really call it sex," Violet said.

"Call it whatever you want," said Kitty.

Violet said, "Are you sure you're okay?"

"Am I okay? What do you think? I've had offers for franchise operations in four states since my issue of *Gossip* hit the stands."

Now Violet remembered why she wanted to talk to Kitty. "I haven't talked to you since the story came out, have I?" she said. "I've talked to you in my mind, so just let me ask. Did we have a conversation about Lucio Bergonzi?"

"No. Of course I think of you and him when I look through the magazine and I see the picture of the two of you laughing. I always thought he had no sense of humor."

Violet felt better already. Finding out about a new man was always like the beginning of an adventure. "I forgot all about him," she said. "I told Freddy I was going to woo him as a client. Then I met Roger and I wooed him. I hope Lucio hasn't signed with another publicist."

"I wouldn't know," Kitty said.

"He's awfully attractive," Violet said. "I thought I'd arrange to run into him at another party soon, have a drink with him, maybe invite him to the wedding. I guess I have to let people know I'm getting married even if they're men.

Helena's giving Alexandra and me a big double wedding reception."

"That's great. There must be an epidemic of marriage fever," Kitty said. "How did I get to be immune?"

Violet said, "Maybe it's the sunspots. Freddy told me they're the reason his temper's been flaring up. Do you believe it?"

"I was never serious about Giorgio," Kitty said, though Violet had discreetly not asked. "I'll be glad if he and Alexandra are divinely happy forever. That way I can forgive them both."

Violet cleared her throat. "I was wondering about the food."

"A double wedding reception is double publicity," Kitty said. "I'll give you the food as your present."

Violet didn't know how to inform her friends without seeming greedy that she wanted silver and crystal for wedding presents. "That's very generous," she said. She lit a cigarette. Inhaling made her light-headed. There didn't seem to be any barrier now between herself and getting married to Philip. She wanted to smoke until smoke filled every cell of her body. "Have you got Lucio's number?" she said.

Kitty said, "I have it at the office, but I don't know if I should give it to you."

Violet said, "I don't know what you're talking about. Philip's the opera lover in our family. Maybe Lucio can get us free seats." And then, since she'd brought the idea into being, she saw how she and Philip and Lucio could be friends. Lucio could become a client, Philip could talk to him about opera and other things he loved, she could flirt without consequences. After she'd gained enough experience she'd write a book on the art of flirting without consequences. By that time, trust her luck, if Rita wasn't still living at home she'd probably be a grandmother. "You'll stay younger longer if you don't get married and have a family," she said to Kitty. She hung up to light the oven because Philip was coming for dinner.

Kitty called Helena from her jasmine bubble bath on Sunday morning to talk things over.

"I was just thinking about where the bandstand should go," Helena said. "Paulo and the Flippers are going to play at my apartment for the big wedding."

Kitty said, "I told Violet I'd give her the wedding feast as a present." She took a pumice stone off the shelf and rubbed the callus on her left foot.

"How about Alexandra?"

"I offered her Aphrodisia, but I think I'll give her the food instead. I'm afraid I'd miss Aphrodisia."

"I'm going to announce my baby at the wedding reception," Helena said. "We can have a big wedding cake with two couples on top, and a small baby cake in the appropriate color."

"You mean I'm going to be the only one without something to celebrate?" Surely, Kitty said to herself, a woman whose shoulders smelled so sweet would soon find a man to console her.

"We could have another cake," Helena said, "shaped like a stack of thousand-dollar bills."

Kitty said, "Everyone's life is changing suddenly. I don't want to be left with nothing but a stack of thousand-dollar bills."

"My life will be entirely changed," said Helena, "but I think of it as a progression. I'm a very visual person. When the baby comes I'll have someone of my own to watch. Hold on a second while I switch to the other ear." Kitty heard the clunk of the receiver being laid down on the telephone table next to the bed. Helena came back on sounding breathless. She said, "There is something I want to tell you about. Roger Rathbone called me yesterday afternoon."

"He didn't."

"He said he couldn't get me out of his head. I told him I was pregnant. He said he loved pregnant women. He said bellies turned him on. I think he wants a child of his own."

"Did you tell him never to call you again?"

"No. I told him he could call me tomorrow," Helena said sweetly. "I love the way he talks. Being on the phone with him was so comfortable, it was as if someone had designed the perfect chair for me, and after standing up for years I finally got to sit down and relax."

Kitty said, "What about John?"

"It's only a telephone romance. A man should be grateful to anyone who can give his wife an inner glow, when she's carrying his baby just to please him."

"No cook lobster—lobster no samba, red hot," Kitty said.

"What?"

"That's a line from 'The Lobster Samba.' "

"I only know the beginning," Helena said.

Kitty said, "You sounded like Violet when you said a man should be grateful to anyone who can give his wife an inner glow."

Helena didn't say anything.

"Anyway," Kitty said, "I called to tell you I'm not mad at you."

"For what?"

"For telling Judy Thaxter how to find my parents."

"I didn't do that. What makes you think I did?"

Poor Helena's voice got thin when she was lying. "You're the only one who knew," Kitty said.

"She probably just looked them up in the phone book."

"Think about it, Helena. How would she know it was the Longpond, Ohio, phone book she wanted?"

"I don't know," Helena said. "Maybe I did do it. At your party for me. I drank so much champagne I remember Judy sitting down with me and I don't remember what happened after that. Nobody can be expected to apologize for what they don't remember."

"I said I wasn't mad," Kitty said.

"That's good," Helena said. "You know, I was thinking, why don't you train Aphrodisia and show her? I'll bet you can meet some interesting men at dog shows."

Kitty said, "Brenda Beatty told me she trained her dog to lick her toes during sex."

"As long as you're not mad," said Helena, "I do have a vague memory of telling Judy where your parents lived. It came to me just the other day, and I'm not sure whether it happened or it was a dream. She said she'd heard they were crazy alcoholics. I thought I was defending your name telling her they were simple farmers."

"You did the right thing," Kitty said. "I'm sorry I chewed your ear off."

"It's okay," said Helena. "I feel better now that I've told you."

Kitty said, "So do I."

Helena liked to have the last word. "Friends are supposed to make you feel better," she said. "That's what friends are for."